PRAISE

"Brooke Dean is an amazing author whose characters leap off the pages. Her imagination is off the chain and the writing is out of the box. A lot of people claim to write erotica, but this is authentic and will have many wanting to test the waters of the BDSM lifestyle by the time they finish reading."

~ Zane, NYT bestselling author, Publisher, Director, and Producer

"*Brooklyn Unbound* is a brilliantly written work of erotica! The perfect mix of sex, self-discovery and the search for connection and community. This book will keep you turning the pages…"

~Leticia S., Amazon Reviewer

A NOVEL

The first edition of *Brooklyn Unbound* was published on June 21, 2022.

Written by Brooke Dean
Published by Brooke D. Dean
www.brookeddean.com

Distributed by IngramSpark

Second printing. February 14, 2024.
ISBN 978-1-962870-14-6

A NOVEL

The first edition of *Brooklyn Unbound* was published on June 21, 2022.

Written by Brooke Dean
Published by Brooke D. Dean
www.brookeddean.com

Distributed by IngramSpark

Second printing. February 14, 2024.
ISBN 978-1-962870-14-6

DEDICATION

For Jaxon, I love you beyond my soul. Thank you for choosing me.

Acknowledgments

Thank you, God. The universe is aligned for my greatest good and I'm so grateful. To my son Jaxon, thank you for loving me. You motivate me to follow my dreams and remind me that it's never too late. You are my best creation and I strive to make you proud every day. Thank you for your patience while I was writing and you wanted to play. You are my heart's joy. Thank you to my mommy, Donna Dean, for raising me, nurturing me, guiding me, and mostly importantly – simply loving me. Your support all my life has inspired me to be the best version of myself. That is all YOU. Thank you to my dad, Bruce Dean, for your love and support. Nicole Dahmani – my other self – there is no me without you. Even though you are my younger sister, I admire and look up to you as the epitome of what a Godly woman, devoted wife, awesome mother and amazing friend should look like. I love you. Fouad, Kyce, Ibrahim, Nadia – My family. I love you and cherish you! To my sisters-in-life, my dear girlfriends who hold me down and lift me up - thank you for the moments of love and laughter that I so desperately needed throughout the years, through my ups and downs and trials and triumphs. The encouragement and support you have given me on a daily basis are what kept me going during this process when I thought I wasn't good enough. It means more than you will ever know.

Brooklyn UNBOUND

A NOVEL

BROOKE DEAN

One

This insomnia shit was getting old.

I can't remember the last time I've slept through the night without waking up sweaty and horny from some dream I had. I couldn't remember everything by the time I gasped awake in the wee hours of the morning. I was acting like some teenage girl with raging hormones she couldn't control instead of a grown-ass woman with a corporate career and bills to pay.

I heave yet another sigh at the ceiling as I lay in bed in the dark, in the same position I've been in for the last couple of hours.

Go... To... Sleep.

My brain and racing thoughts ignore my commands as they have since I first woke up. *God, I'm so exhausted.* One of my subordinates actually felt bold enough to call out the dark circles carved under my eyes at work the other day, and that's not a good look for a boss.

Hot frustration surges through me and I stretch out my arm to grab my cell on my nightstand.

I tap the screen to wake it up and squint at the time. *4:40 A.M.* Too early to get up and start my day, but too late for another attempt at some real restorative sleep.

Whatever.

I turn on the nightlight and drag my laptop towards me from its resting spot on the other side of my large bed. The empty space it occupied reminds me once again of how devoid of male company I am at the moment.

My fingers fly over the keyboard as I try to distract myself with the blogs I visit on the regular.

No new celebrity gossip. In ten minutes, I'm already over it.

A thought, a persistent one that has been nagging me for weeks now, slithers to the front of my mind. I know exactly what I want to research, but… I feel my cheeks catch fire in the silence of my bedroom, despite the fact that I'm obviously the only one present in my apartment.

Throat suddenly dry, I swallow hard, my hands poised over the keyboard once more. I'll die if anyone in my life ever finds out about this new… inclination I've learned that I have.

Opening a private tab on my browser to conceal my search history for good measure – just in case anyone ever gets a hold of my laptop, like the Feds, or something – I type in my query and hit "enter."

My eyes widen at the literal *millions* of search results.

BDSM lifestyle.

BDSM forum boards.

How to start a BDSM lifestyle.

BDSM lifestyle for newbs.

Well, damn.

Part of me feels validated by the sheer number of people seemingly into the darker side of sex. Most of me still feels a deep, unutterable shame for even looking it up; especially for the reason why I felt the need in the first place.

I realized it back when my ex would frequently (try) to blow my back out. He had a reasonably thick tool to work with, but I still could never get there, no matter how tender he was or how hard he hit my cervix from the back. Then one night, out of nowhere, he unintentionally tweaked my arm behind me so hard he hurt my shoulder and the pain somehow made me cum so hard I blacked out for a couple of seconds.

Never in my life had I experienced something like that. He was *so* proud, but I knew the truth. And I had to break up with him because I also realized that something had to be wrong with me.

Figured I might as well see if this… *thing* that's taken hold of me has a name.

I click on a random forum board and start reading through entry after entry, noting with a smirk that the names of all the contributors seem to be anonymized. I'm not the only one trying to hide.

I understand next to nothing about all this, so I read for another hour or so, gleaning what I can to try and make sense of what I felt in that twisted moment of ecstasy all those months ago.

Just reading about the naughty experiences of a thousand strangers gets me so worked up, I can barely see straight. I set my laptop aside and slide out of bed, my inner thighs slick under my satin nighty due to my wetness.

My morning routine starts on autopilot; my thoughts are somewhere else entirely as I pee, shower and brush my teeth.

When had this happened? At what point did my subconscious mind and my body decide that they required pain to produce the synergy required for a mind- blowing orgasm?

It's true that I have a few daddy issues, but no more than the next upwardly mobile woman in New York City. I can't see how any of that could relate to my suddenly being intrigued at the prospect of being hog-tied and pile-driven simultaneously.

I shake my head at myself in the mirror as I dab soapy water off my face with a hand towel. *Christ, what's happening to me?*

And speaking of the son of God, what would my church congregation think of me if they knew I was into this level of kink?

Shuddering at the mere thought, I hurry into some comfy clothes for the day, spritz on a bit of casual floral perfume, and make my way into my apartment kitchen.

I almost burn my scrambled eggs, I'm so distracted. Every time I think of the sexual scenarios I read about this morning, I imagine myself in them with a faceless man that is rippling with muscle and masculine pheromones. Just the thought of being tied to some apparatus with my legs spread as far as they will stretch, blindfolded and unable to move, screaming until my throat is raw while said man sucks all my juices into his mouth…

A pang of pure, unadulterated desire pulses through my core and throughout my body, so intense I drop my spatula on the stove and spatter myself with melted butter from the skillet. Great.

But before I run back to my bedroom to change, I decide to pause, just for a second. What would be so bad about giving in to the fantasy, to try it on for size? No one else is here. Who would know I was dabbling in a little depravity?

Holding on to the edge of the granite countertop, I close my eyes and let myself feel what I had been resisting all morning. Mentally, I float back to the gentleman in my mind, who now has me tied in such a way that my face is down on the hard ground and my ass is up in the air.

A moan works its way up my throat and my eyes snap back open. Mystery man in my head hasn't even touched me yet and I've already soaked through my panties. Now I need to change for more reasons than one.

This might be deeper than I previously thought.

I slide my eggs onto a plate and throw a couple of pieces of bread into the toaster before I dash back into my room to raid my panty drawer for a dry pair. By the time I hear my toast pop up, I'm in a fresh top and back in the kitchen.

I'm not even hungry. Still, I deliberately take my plate to the table because I know my stomach will start growling as I run my errands today if I don't eat, and that's humiliating for an adult.

My eyes catch a glimpse of the outdoors since I forgot to close the blinds last night. The morning looks so inviting, with the vivid green of my potted plants stacked around the perimeter of the balcony in stark contrast to the powdery blue of the clear sky. Maybe taking my breakfast outside for a change will help clear my head a little. And perhaps take my mind off the distracting arousal still pounding between my legs.

I grab my phone off the kitchen table where I'd left it and head outside with my plate, using my hip against the large handle to push the sliding glass door out of my way.

The eggs and dry toast – I forgot the butter and I'm too tired to drag myself back to the fridge to get it – taste like ash in my mouth. All I can think about is my swollen lady parts being spanked with a paddle.

My ringer goes off and I almost jump out of my skin. I narrowly miss dropping it on the concrete ground as I fumble to answer.

"Hello?"

I recognize my friend's breathy giggle before she speaks. "I don't know why you sound so surprised I'm calling."

Rolling my eyes, I stuff another forkful of lukewarm eggs into my mouth.

"Good morning, Sherry."

"It'll be a good morning if you actually come to church with me today. You haven't shown your face in weeks."

I keep chewing to suppress a groan, still tasting nothing. I *really* don't feel like going to church today. I need… I don't know, time. Time to figure out what's happening to me without some kind of obligation hanging over my head.

Ridiculous? Probably, but I'm not up to being around a bunch of pious people today when I'm already riddled with guilt and feeling as dirty as a week-old dishrag.

Sherry must have recognized my reticence as a precursor to a decline to her invitation.

"Don't you dare say no, Brook. You promised *weeks* ago that you'd come help me teach Sunday school and then you ghosted me." She giggles. "Now you know that's heathen behavior not befitting a child of God."

A chuckle bubbles up before I can stop it. She sounds exactly like the oldest deaconess of the church who loves looking down her nose at everyone.

I lean back in my deck chair and answer her with a longsuffering sigh.

"I guess I can drag myself down there this morning, but only because I like you."

"Well, hopefully you like the Lord, too."

Knowing Sherry is a "reformed slut" by her own admission, I nod and say, "Mmh-hmm."

"Anyway, Brother Anthony is gonna be really happy to see you today. He asks about you every time I see him. It's almost annoying."

I hum something in acknowledgement and Sherry takes it as a cue to spout a list of attributes of a man I'll never be interested in, but I've put her on speaker to fiddle with my cell. I'd come across a list of apps on one of the forum boards I'd visited earlier that piqued my curiosity. What was the name of it? BDSM World, or something…

I try that as a search stream and find it among several others. My heart suddenly racing, I wait for it to download while Sherry gabs on, unaware that I haven't said anything in several minutes.

"Are you listening to me?"

"Yeah, girl," I say, biting my lip as I set up an account and fill out my profile, wondering if I should use a real photo of myself. Probably not a good idea…

"Well, what do you think? Would you be willing to go out with him?"

Huh?

"Go out with who?"

"With Anthony! I've been talking about him since we got on the phone… I knew you weren't listening." Sherry huffs. "What are you doing, anyway? Since you clearly aren't paying *me* any attention."

"I'm sorry, Sher. Just distracted by this… ah, dating app I just downloaded, that's all."

I've known Sherry since we were coworkers at a previous job more than a decade ago, but I still don't feel comfortable enough to tell her what *kind* of dating app I'm scrolling through. I don't plan on telling anybody. Ever.

"Why didn't you say that? Nobody wants you to end your dry spell more than I do."

We both giggle… especially me, since I wasn't dry at all a little bit ago.

"Do you see anybody promising?"

That's an understatement if I ever heard one. I can't believe how many different types of men pop up that fit my profile preferences, in every shade, musclebound and beefy, or slim and chiseled, with detailed bios that are downright scandalous.

I keep swiping, blushing furiously. "Um, a few," I tell Sherry, trying to keep my voice light despite the fact that my hands are suddenly trembling.

I can feel myself swelling, opening, getting more and more wet the longer I sit there reading about the desires of these gorgeous men and imagining myself exactly the way they would want me – bound, gagged, begging, and ready to be pounded into sweet, sweet oblivion.

Shit. It feels like someone lit a fire between my legs.

"Hey, what's wrong?"

I must have let out a moan without realizing it, and if I had, even I didn't know if it was borne of sexual frustration or despair.

"Uh, nothing. Hey, Sherry… I'm going to go ahead and get ready for church, okay? I'll see you there, I promise."

"You'd better. I'll meet you out front."

We sign off and I refocus on the app that has my heart thumping so hard. I haven't even talked to anyone and I'm already more turned on than I can remember being in years.

Still gnawing my lip, I wonder at myself if I dare to do what I'm thinking of doing in this exact moment.

My chest is heaving. Fantasies built from the spicy profile descriptions of man after man play on a string in my mind, vivid enough to make me break a sweat. Oh, God. Church is the last thing on my mind right now.

Equal parts nervous and excited, I glance all around to see if any of my neighbors are lurking on their balconies. I see no one to my left or right or directly above me. My apartment is high enough from the ground floor that no one would be able to see me from below. All of this, in addition to the way my potted plant garden has thickened over the winter to create a shady cocoon, makes for a pretty private moment.

Private enough for me to do the unthinkable.

Still seated, I wriggle out of my damp panties and toss them onto the empty chair next to me. I prop a leg up on the same chair and part my thighs, letting my head fall back and my eyes close against the morning sunlight that warms my skin.

I can see a man in my mind's eye, a single entity cobbled together from fragments of the men I've discovered on the app this morning. He is everything I ever dreamed of, and he wants to fulfill my every dark, dangerous fantasy without the judgment I always fear.

My hand becomes an extension of him, soft and tender, as fingers caress their way down the column of my neck, across my collarbones, curve around and under the heavy globe of a breast contained within my lacy bra. I almost whip it off but the desire train is already roaring down the track, my hand – his hand – skirting lower and lower, down my flat stomach and over the pronounced curve of my hip.

I'm breathless, waiting for him to reach where I need his touch the most. My fingers find me hot and aching, slick down to my inner thighs like I had been when I awoke from my forgotten dreams.

A soft moan escapes me. I stroke, my movements slow and deliberate, letting my fantasy man take his time exploring the depths of my neediness.

My fingers reach deeper, bottoming out in my womanhood as I gasp. I know what I want.

My hips begin to buck against the hand between my legs on their own, but I'm so aroused at this point, I hardly care that I've nearly bumped my half-eaten plate off the table.

My fantasy man is choking me now, firm hands gripping my throat as he pounds into me from behind so fast it feels as if his thrusts are knocking against my sternum.

When he smacks my ass, again and again, my full cheeks ripple against the firm strike of his hand, leaving me sore and wanting more. So much more.

I want him to choke me harder.

Leave imprints of his huge hands on my reddened flesh.

Humiliate me.

Make me beg.

Shoot the thick essence of his manhood down my throat so forcefully I choke and ask for more.

I'm only half-aware of my hand moving so fast it's a blur. The hot pleasure swirling in my body begins to coalesce at a peak that threatens to dismantle me from the inside out.

As I imagine the man in my head swiping his thickness across my wet and waiting lips before smacking my jaw hard enough to hurt, a wave of disgust at myself drowns out the rising ecstasy that had been curling around the base of my spine.

God, I can't believe I have stooped this low, diddling myself in full public view for anyone to gawk at if they had half a mind to, all while getting off on imagining a stranger degrading me.

My eyes blink open to the cloudless blue sky yawning wide above me. My hand slows but it's still moving; though the intensity of my need has ebbed, I'm still too close to the finish line to make myself stop now.

I hover on the edge, pumping my fingers as a sense of desperation sets in. I can't get there. Just like with my ex.

With that thought comes the solution. I strum the plump bud between my lips with one hand and dig the manicured fingernails of the other into my opposite thigh as hard as I can without drawing blood.

And, like before, it's the spark of pain that finally catapults me over the edge.

I cry out, the pleasure cresting hard enough to arch my back in the chair and make me slap my dry hand over my mouth to stifle my howl of relief. The peak is over nearly as soon as it starts, hollow and unsatisfying.

The disappointment and shame that settles over me then are as keen as the fleeting pleasure had been.

Something is seriously wrong with me.

The remnants of bliss fade and I right myself in the chair, my face steaming hot at the idea that I may have had an audience for my... indiscretion.

Tapping the screen of my phone to check the time again, I realize I'll have to hurry if I didn't want to miss Sunday School and risk hearing Sherry complain about it the whole morning service.

I clean up my plate and throw everything in the sink, leaving the dishes for later. After tossing on a knit dress, sliding into some practical heels and grabbing my purse and keys, I'm out of the door and trying to forget what the hell came over me outside on the balcony.

I can't understand how perusing that app made me feel worse instead of better. Even as the doorman smiles and greets me as I step outside, I wonder if the quality of his acknowledgement would change if he knew what I had been up to and why.

At least the crisp air perks me up a bit as I make my way into the bustling Manhattan crowds that are already packing the sidewalk early Sunday morning. My feet quickly fall into that distinctive New York cadence as we all rush to our important destinations of the day.

Although I usually don't make eye contact, I find myself catching the gaze of a stranger here and there, wondering if I can see evidence of sexual deviance in their eyes alone. Maybe the white guy in the suit over there likes to have his balls stepped on by a sexy woman in high heels. Or maybe the woman in the church dress enjoys slobbering on the dicks of strange men through a hole in the wall of a public restroom. I suppose no one really knows what goes on behind the closed doors of friends and family.

Yes, it's stupid, but it somehow makes me feel less alone. Scrolling through a specific app with thousands of members around the world simply doesn't feel the same.

Sometimes I wonder if this need of mine that has recently surfaced has been lurking in the background of my relationships all this time. Perhaps that's why I was never satisfied for long with one guy, no matter how enamored I was with him at the beginning. There was always a nagging little itch in the back of my mind.

I still don't know for sure if I'm brave enough to scratch it.

Hanging a right at the intersection, I cross the street, shoulder to shoulder with my walking partners, a cool breeze slipping through the spaces between the throng.

I look down the street and see the block down the way where the television network I practically run looms over all who pass by. Okay, maybe *run* is an exaggeration, but as a producer I know my network couldn't move forward efficiently without me.

The youngest primetime producer in the entire history of the network. That's me, and I'm as proud of that fact as I have every right to be, as hard as I've worked for it. I've had my professional life figured out since I was a senior in high school. Too bad things on the personal side of my world are murky as ever.

I've asked myself if a long-term relationship is something I actually want more times than I can count at this point. It has occurred to me that I may just *think* I want it because society tells me – tells everyone - that I should. Still, the thought of being untethered in this world and alone forever fills me with the kind of dread that can keep a woman up at night.

Hardly anyone pays me any attention during the twenty-minute walk to the Baptist church in my neighborhood, but I still feel like I have a scarlet letter "A" stitched to the back of my dress by the time I arrive.

"As I live and breathe, Brooklyn."

I grin. Sherry is waiting for me on the steps that lead up to the old stone building, her thick arms crossed over her chest. My eyes widen at the amount of her ample cleavage she has allowed to show under her classy suit. I guess old habits are hard to break? "I almost can't believe you showed up."

Smirking, I walk up to meet her and she envelopes me in a brief hug. "I told you I would."

"Yeah, yeah." Her soft hand pats my cheek and a smile stretches across her face, revealing the considerable gap between her teeth. I've always thought it makes her look charming. "It's good to see you, Brookie."

I don't know why I tend to withdraw from my friends whenever I find myself in the midst of some kind of turmoil. It never fails to surprise me how much better I tend to feel about things once I'm in their presence, especially Sherry. She's always a fluffy bundle of sarcastic joy.

Even with a friend at my side in a familiar setting, I still feel like a poser in he midst of a congregation I've known for years. Folks I haven't seen in a long while greet me as I follow Sherry up the aisle and head for the back of the church, where the small classrooms are kept.

I tack a bright smile to my face all through Sunday School; when I act out the voices of the Bible story I'm teaching on, the little kids laughing at my feet have no idea that my guilt has been building to critical mass deep in my gut and I can barely breathe.

Sherry settles in next to me during the sermon, closer than usual. Part of me wonders if she's trying to keep an eye on me to make sure I don't bolt or something, but I decide not to make a fuss.

"Church," the pastor begins in his gravelly voice, already dabbing sweat from his brow with a handkerchief, "today I wanna talk to y'all about your secret sin."

Oh, shit – ugh, I shouldn't even *think* curse words right now.

I knew this would happen. The second I sit myself down in front of this pastor, he starts preaching a sermon that sounds like it was custom-made for me.

I want to roll my eyes at the Lord, but I manage to resist.

Try as I might to pay attention to what I need to hear, my mind is already wandering. My eyes rove the crowd and happen to catch a dark brown set staring right back at me, attached to a broad, mustached smile. Ah, Brother Anthony. He looks like he's been waiting for me to catch his glance for a while now.

The smile I return is polite but not exactly warm. He's a little too thirsty for my taste. Always too eager. Plus, his moustache looks like a dead caterpillar the way it sort of… sits there atop his lip. Sherry is a fan but I can't see myself being with him. There's no way he can get it.

Looking away quickly, a suited gentleman wearing a thick belt with a huge buckle moseys his way down the main aisle back to his seat, presumably from a visit to the restroom at the rear of the main sanctuary.

He certainly made a statement with that thing. You could tie someone up with it as surely as handcuffs. Make them do all kinds of things and they would be totally helpless…

I almost gasp at the tremendous left turn my thoughts have taken. Or maybe I really did, if the side eye I received from Sherry is any indication.

Taking a deep breath, I pinch my eyes closed. I need to get a grip.

As I reopen my eyes and look up at the gigantic empty crucifix bolted to the opposite wall, I try my best to settle my guilty heart and mind.

I should be visualizing the sacrifice of Christ. Instead, all I can see is an image of my most naked self, strapped down to that same cross, spread-eagled and screaming while some sexy ass man takes his pleasure from my body, until I'm flooding him with my juices –

"Are you okay?" Sherry leans over to whisper in my ear, concern etched on her brow. "You look pale as a ghost. Is your blood sugar low?"

Shaken, I pat her hand and whisper back, trying to avoid the preaching pastor's attention. "I'm fine. Just a little indigestion, I think."

She raises an eyebrow but doesn't question me. Which is a pity, because I absolutely need to be questioned by someone with sense right now, considering the fact that I'm sure to leave a wet spot on the pew cushion at this point.

I clasp my hands together into a tight ball in my lap and try to will away the arousal that has me caught tightly in its grip. After all the sexcapades and "hoetations" of my (sometimes) misspent youth, I have never had an issue keeping my focus in the house of the Lord before today. A sexy memory might have flitted across my mind now and then, but I have always been able to extinguish them the second they appeared.

Now I'm having depraved fantasies while sitting in the middle of the congregation, packed onto a pew with my fellow man, under the wary eye of a pastor who would probably drown me in holy water if he knew what was on my mind.

I thought I had handled this earlier on my balcony! My stomach churns bile at knowing my wanton display of indecency was for nothing.

If anything, my erotic fire is burning hotter in this moment than it ever has before.

Shifting to find a more comfortable position, I clear my throat and squint at the pastor pacing the pulpit in the throes of his sermon. God, I wish I could pay attention to what he's saying.

No matter what I do, I can't find a position on the stupid pew that doesn't leave me feeling exposed and sinful. For the next hour I make a point to ignore the intermittent stare I receive from Sherry, hot as a brand on the side of my face.

The instant the choir members rise to their feet in the stands beyond the pulpit, I know freedom is at hand.

"If there be anyone present today among you that wants to be free from their burden of iniquity, let them come now to the altar for God's grace and salvation."

My ass needs to be throwing myself at the pastor's feet, but I don't dare move beyond clapping my trembling hands in support of those who come forward with their heads hung low.

The same heartbeat that is racing in my ears and chest is positively pounding at the juncture of my thighs and I know I am on the edge of losing it.

Would I go directly to Hell if I made a beeline for the ladies' room and rubbed one out? God, I should be so ashamed of myself.

The pastor speaks the last words of the final prayer and a gentle wave of relief flows over me, for an instant.

Escape!

My feet are already moving quickly across the faded carpet toward the double doors, but the sense of remorse that settles deep into my gut like a lump of lead slows my pace.

No, I need to stick around, especially since I appear to be turning into some kind of sexual deviant. I need to be near all these imperfect people who are trying hard every day to make their lives better, to conquer their lesser natures. Mine seems to be winning right now, but… maybe it didn't always have to be this way.

Church members I hadn't seen in some time come up to greet me one after another, all smiles, as pleased to see me as if I had been here every single Sunday for the last two months instead of being MIA.

A little boy I've taught a few times in Sunday School runs up and hugs my legs before running off into the church parking lot to find his friends. My heart warms deep inside my chest as I watch the kid interact so easily with everyone around him, guileless and sweet with the innocence of youth.

I swallow hard. I *have* to get rid of that app.

The app, the forum boards — all of it needs to go. Anything that has anything to do with BDSM and the lifestyle associated with it needs to be out of my life. And especially out of my head, where it's most dangerous.

I don't know what I was thinking. Looking around at the smiling faces of everyone in no hurry to leave brings back the happy glow of community I hadn't realized I was missing.

Perhaps a "normal" relationship with a normal kind of guy who wants to be a part of such a community is what I need to focus on. What if Sherry is right and Brother Anthony is exactly the kind of man I need?

"Sister Brooklyn, I thought that was you."

Speak of the devil… though the saint would be more accurate in this case.

My fingers find a loose curl that has escaped my bun and tuck it behind my ear.

"Uh… hello, Anthony. Haven't seen you in a while. How are you?"

I try to look him in his dark eyes but he's too… intense. I offer my brightest smile, even if I can't exactly make eye contact at the moment.

"Well, I'm a lot better, now that I've seen *you* today."

The urge to roll my eyes is strong, but I valiantly resist. Honestly, I saw that line coming a mile away… is he seriously trying to flirt with me with such weak game?

I decide to indulge him. For the moment, at least. He can't possibly become the man of my dreams if I don't give him a chance out of the gate.

I bat my eyes and say, "Glad I could be of service."

Even I'm not sure what I mean by that, but Anthony smiles down at me from his considerable height and doesn't seem phased by my ambiguity. He might even think it's cute.

He starts trying to make conversation and I'm disappointed in myself to find that I've already checked out mentally. I stare at him and nod, discreetly trying to study him. I'd love to understand why I do not find myself attracted to this kind, respectful, church-going man – a man I know without a doubt would treat me right and bring me home to meet his mama as soon as he possibly could.

His locs are shoulder-length and tied into a neat bundle at the nape of his neck, and the fit of his navy-blue suit suggests there is some muscle under all that fabric that is outside of public view. Still… something about him makes the juiciness I've been plagued with all morning begin to dry up like the Sahara.

I notice he's staring with an expectant look on his face and get a sinking feeling.

"Did… did you hear what I said?"

This isn't going well at all…

"Sorry," I say with wide eyes, cheeks heating under his steady gaze. "I didn't catch it. Still a little loud in here."

He smiles yet another benign smile at me and appears to take my lame excuse in stride.

I force my lips to grin and try to look interested and confused at the same time.

"I said that I think we should grab a coffee or something soon. I know of a lot of really great places nearby. Would you like that, Brooklyn?"

Not likely, but I don't have the heart to tell him that. I may be more interested in delving into the dark underbelly of society than continuing this conversation, but I'm not an outright asshole. I can be nice.

My hand reaches out to give his arm a friendly pat, but I draw it back the instant I realize it might give him false hope and the wrong impression.

"I'm usually pretty busy, but maybe! That does sound nice." I start pushing my way through the crowd toward the entrance again.

Anthony follows on my heels but falls behind as a couple of people squeeze in between us on their way out.

"Don't you think I should get your number, then?"

I really don't, so I pretend not to hear him and start to veer left toward the restrooms, giving him a friendly wave before I disappear inside.

After I do my business, I ponder over Anthony while I wash my hands to avoid having to study myself too closely in the mirror. He hardly makes my skin crawl and is decent to look at. I suppose it could be his lack of imagination that rubs me the wrong way. He never seems to think outside of the box or color outside the lines. In fact, I don't think his wardrobe contains any colors beyond brown and navy. I'd be bored of him in 24 hours, and that wouldn't be fair to either of us.

Better to be congenial, yet aloof. Shouldn't be too difficult, as long as I can keep Sherry out of my business.

As I push open the door to leave the restroom, I hear my phone ding in my purse. Probably Sherry, trying to see where I ended up after disappearing into the sea of humanity that was the outgoing church congregation.

I pause and grab my cell, lips pursed as I check out my recent notifications. And oh yes, that reminds me that I need to delete that app –

Oh, wait.

That notification was from *BDSM Life*.

My breathing stutters and my hands begin to tremble.

My back hits the tiled wall behind the door in a spot that is safely out of the way.

I log in.

I hold my breath.

Jesus Christ!

One profile match.

Fear stalls the finger that hovers over the inbox button.

Part of me wants to pray for strength, but I know God has nothing to do with this.

I never expected to be matched at all, let alone so quickly! It's only been on my phone for a few hours and there's already someone potentially knocking at my virtual door? Are they male or female? What do they want from me – my body or my will?

Or both?

My hand drops to my side, still clutching my phone. I try to force some air back into my lungs.

Get a grip, Brooklyn.

It's not a big deal.

It's *not* a big deal. It's a stupid app full of hot men with questionable ethics and women with daddy issues. I am intimately familiar with the latter.

I snort a laugh at my stupidity in this moment. I am a television producer! Crises of all kinds are my daily bread and butter. I can handle anything.

Time to stop being a pussy.

I open the app message before I can talk myself out of it again.

Hi B,

I can tell even from your tiny profile pic that you are gorgeous beyond words. I'd love a chance to get to know you if you're ever interested in chatting. Hit me up.

- J

He sounds… normal. Not gross in the least, although he surely must be, but I've had to entertain sleazier come-ons by regular guys in corporate environments.

I bite my lip. A chat couldn't hurt, right? A chat is *harmless.*

No way am I deleting this app now.

Sorry, Lord.

Two

I'm still holding my breath, trying to decide how I should respond to my new mysterious digital suitor – or if I should at all – when the restroom door swings open and I have to put my hands up to keep from breaking my nose against the peeling wood. I thought I was safely out of the way, but it wasn't the best place to stand in hindsight.

I lose my death grip on my phone and it clatters to the floor in the process.

"What – oh, I'm so sorry… Brooklyn? What are you doing hiding behind the door?"

Sherry has tracked me down, apparently. I scoop up my phone with a wince, hoping the thick protector I've recently bought did its job and the screen didn't crack against the tile.

"I wasn't hiding," I say.

"Sure, you weren't," Sherry says with a smirk, already moving toward an empty stall.

Sometimes I wish she didn't know me so well.

Satisfied that my phone is largely unscathed, I drop it back into my purse. Something tells me I'm not going to have time to deal with the app right now. Sherry had that sparkle in her eye that usually indicates she has something up her sleeve and plans to drag me into it.

"I was looking for you, anyway," Sherry called across the restroom after she flushed, confirming my suspicions. In the mirror above the sink where she washes her hands, she catches my gaze over her shoulder. I arrange my face to look pleasantly surprised and interested.

"What's going on?" I smile and nod at one of the ladies who waves at me as she exits.

"So, a few of us are going to brunch to catch up, and I wanted to ask if you wanted to go." She waggles her eyebrows at me. "Anthony said he was going."

I swallow my grunt. I bet he jumped at that invitation, knowing Sherry and I are friends.

It isn't as if I'm not hungry, considering my paltry breakfast experience at home.

"And whose idea was this exactly?" I cock an eyebrow so she knows I'm on to her trickery. And meddling, for that matter.

She at least has the decency to look bashful. "Fine… it was mine. I worry about you, Brook. You've been so distant lately, I wanted to make sure you could hang out with people who care about you."

Well, that took a serious turn. My heart warms at the sincerity of Sherry's words and expression. Now I can't possibly say no, even if I wanted to.

I catch the barest glint of mischief in her eyes right before I scowl at her. "This feels like a setup," I say and she bursts out laughing, cleavage jiggling and thick curls bouncing around her round face.

"Maybe a little. I mean, how often do I get to see you? Besides, I am so tired of hearing you complain to me on the phone that there aren't any good men in New York when one is waiting for us outside right now."

I heave a long, theatrical sigh and study the water stains on the ceiling tiles. "Fine. I guess I could eat… but you are absolutely paying for it, since you want to ambush me with a date."

"Whatever. Just don't order the steak."

I laugh and Sherry rolls her eyes before linking her arm with mine and pulling me after her into the main hallway. She lets me go and I follow her outside onto the stone steps of the church.

Sucking on a cigarette like her life depended on it is Katrina Livingston, a three-time divorcee with five children who is nearly a decade younger than myself. She smiles when she sees me, but she still has that look to her like she is a few seconds from jumping on the nearest subway and skipping town for good. My personal life might be a little iffy at the moment, but at least I don't have to deal with that kind of stress.

Standing next to her is a woman who appeared closer to my age, clothed in a dress that looked like she strutted straight from the club to church service this morning. Having never seen her before, I make my introductions and shake her hand.

"Paulette," she says with a snap of the gum she's chewing. She looks down her nose at me after her limp handshake and picks up her conversation with Katrina again.

I shoot Sherry a look like WTF? and she shrugs.

"Hello, again."

I look up to find Anthony standing right next to me as if he's appeared from the ether. Giggling nervously, I duck my head. His mere presence ushers in a wave of guilt over what I'm hiding in my purse.

Taking a deep breath, I resolve to make the most of this unexpected afternoon outing. "I guess this situation is better than coffee."

This time, now that I've forced my usual reservations to the rear of my mind, the warmth of Anthony's demeanor actually reaches me and I find myself starting to relax.

"What a blessed day for me," he says with a wink.

I'm so surprised by his boldness, the smile that sneaks up on me is my most genuine yet.

Sherry insists that our small party head to an eatery that opened recently that's supposed to have the best chicken and waffles in Manhattan, not to mention the best bottomless mimosas.

Well, I've wined and dined at the best restaurants in the city, so I decide to reserve judgement until I can sample the goods. And I was dead serious about ordering the most expensive thing on the menu since Messy Sherry said she was treating.

It's close enough to walk, so the four of us set off down the block. Katrina and Paulette continue to chit chat about no-good men and fall in behind Sherry. Anthony hangs back to walk at my side.

He's way closer than what I'd consider appropriate, his arm gently bumping mine time and again as we move down the perpetually crowded sidewalk. It could be the way the late morning sun enhanced the rainbow hues of fruit piled in boxes at the small market stands we pass, or the warm scent of baking *pastelitos* floating on the breeze, but I don't mind him too much at the moment.

"I'm glad we have a chance to talk." Anthony glances at me sideways, waiting for some kind of affirmation from me.

I keep staring ahead. I remind myself of my need to straddle the line that is ever present in my mind: I need to be as aloof as I am polite, always.

"Sure, Anthony."

For a moment as we continue our moderate pace and our party weaves through pedestrians headed the opposite direction, all I hear is the soundtrack of the street – honking horns, snippets of loud conversations in every language under the sun, the squawking of birds fighting over trash in puddles – until Anthony's rumbling voice fills my ears again.

"So, you're a big-time TV producer, right?"

So, he knows where I work – that's common knowledge at church. Not that impressive. "Something like that," I say, watching a flock of pigeons zoom by overhead.

"Was that something you're passionate about, or is it just a 'nine to five'? I've always wanted to ask you."

Now, that response earns my entire focus and I turn to regard him. His open expression suggests he genuinely wants to know if I love my job. Interesting.

"I'm definitely passionate about it." I smile in spite of myself. I can't help it. "It's challenging on the best days and feels downright impossible on the worst ones, but I'm never bored. I solve problems on the fly for the network and nearly everyone who works for it. I'm good at my job because I love it and vice versa."

"That's a beautiful thing." Anthony nods his approval.

"Thanks. I think so, too. Makes it a lot easier to make a living that way."

It takes me a full minute of his silence to realize I haven't asked anything about him.

"And what is it you do again, Anthony?"

"I'm an elementary school principal."

My eyes widen. "Really?"

"Yeah." His eyebrows rise and he gives a little laugh. "Is that so hard to believe?"

"No – not at all." My hand unconsciously finds the back of my neck and rubs at it as I try to hide my embarrassment. "I'm sorry; I didn't mean it like that. It's not a very common profession for… ah…"

"People who look like you and me, you mean," Anthony says, finishing my unspoken thought.

Feeling the first real sense of admiration, I nod with a surprised grin. "Yeah. Exactly that." What a difference a real conversation makes when one takes the time.

"I imagine you understand what it's like to be one of the 'few and proud', so to speak."

A bark of incredulous laughter escapes me at such an understatement. "Oh, most definitely. I was one of a mere handful in my graduating class and still the only black person, let alone woman, in any kind of management position at the network."

"Impressive," Anthony says, "but I'm not at all surprised."

The unexpected praise makes me blush in earnest. I hazard a glance up – way up – at him. "I appreciate that."

A guy dragging a snack cart tries to push his way up the sidewalk and Anthony's huge hand finds the small of my back and gently pushes me out of the way before we continue walking for another few beats of silence.

Just when I'm thinking that agreeing to brunch wasn't such a bad idea after all, Anthony is turning to me again with more questions brewing behind his espresso-brown eyes.

"Hopefully you won't find this to be too forward, but is a family something you want to have one day?"

Talk about getting to the point. Had any other man asked me such an abrupt and invasive question, I would be done altogether and moved on to greener conversational pastures. But Anthony seems to be genuinely kind and interested in what I have to say, so I take the bait.

"I do want a family," I say. At least, I think I do. The trickle of self-doubt triggered by a reminder of my ongoing existential crisis reminds me – once again – of the infamous app I have yet to delete. Not sure how a husband and kids would fit into a world full of whips and chains and handcuffs. "I think I still have a few more years to decide if that's the direction I want my life to go."

Anthony hums, but I can't tell if it's a simple acknowledgement or an agreement.

I throw the same question back at him and he answers quickly as our group follows Sherry around the corner. "If I had my way, I'd already have a family. I'm trying to make sure it's with the right person."

The way he says it and the look he gives me suggests he already has a certain someone in mind.

Feeling bold, I dare to ask: "And what would make her the right person?"

I'm not imagining it; Anthony has moved closer to me. His arm brushes mine nearly every step now.

"A love for God and His people, a desire for children, a commitment to family and home."

There it is. The last part of what he said sets my Spidey senses tingling.

"And – in your view – can a wife commit to family and home as well as a career?" My eyes narrow at him. I need to know if Anthony's old-fashioned veneer matches his worldview.

"I expect my wife to devote herself to our family without having her attentions divided."

Anthony's jaw clenches and I know then there would be no changing his mind on the subject, even if I cared to do it.

I don't know why I'm a little disappointed. I suppose I enjoyed feeling normal for a few fleeting moments and am sad to see it end so quickly.

Any chance of a budding romance between the two of us Anthony just nipped in its very tiny bud. There's no way I'd ever give up my career for something else I wanted, and no man would ever ask me to squash that part of myself for him or anyone else. At least, no man of *mine*. I work hard, I work smart, and I would be damned if I couldn't have it all.

I think I deserve it. I *know* I do.

I also think Anthony can tell that I've checked out emotionally. He looks resigned when I speak up. "Well, I certainly hope you find what you're looking for."

"Thanks for that."

We're quiet the rest of the walk to the restaurant, and I'm okay with it. What else is there to say?

There's a line out of the door when we finally arrive at our destination, so I slowly and politely begin to ease my way toward the other ladies in our group without being too obvious that I'm leaving Anthony's side with intention.

Paulette is a surly one but turns out to be quite the comedienne, leaving all of us in stitches with one story after another about her wild and crazy upbringing in the Bronx with her many siblings. It makes my Pennsylvania childhood with my little brother and sister seem like a church cakewalk in comparison with Paulette's gleeful brushes with the law.

It's well after noon by the time we're seated. Anthony spent the better part of the hour we waited talking up Katrina, so I'm surprised when he goes out of his way to settle into the seat next to me at our table on the open patio.

He catches my curious glance and gives a shrug.

Well, if he doesn't have an issue with me, I'm not about to make one. A dimpled waitress with hips as wide as our table saunters up to us and announces, "Before you even ask, we're out of chicken *and* waffles."

A collective grumble erupts from the five of us.

Paulette smacks her plastic menu down on the wooden tabletop. "Damn! That's the only thing I wanted." She pouts, the childish look on her face at odds with the deep crinkles around her eyes, and I almost laugh aloud. "Just bring me a bloody Mary, then. Shit."

She may be willing to forgo food altogether, but I'm sure as hell not. My growling stomach gives an audible rallying cry as I scan my own menu. I end up ordering a crab cake benedict. A scowling Sherry and Katrina place their orders as well, complaining all the while. The ever-congenial Anthony places his order with none of their fuss, but everyone perks up when Sherry orders bottomless mimosas for the table.

As we wait for our food to be delivered, my brunch companions fall into their own conversations around me. I chuckle to myself listening to them, enjoying the feeling of being exactly where I'm supposed to be. At least for the moment.

Then I hear a ding from my purse hanging over the arm of my chair.

My entire body tenses.

No, I'm *not* going to grab my phone and check the app I know I'm not supposed to be checking, and I'm certainly *not* going to do it at a table full of people.

The mimosas arrive well before the food does. I take a small sip every time I think of checking my phone. Then I realize the alcohol is only making me want to grab my phone more than before. Plus, I might be a little tipsy since I can't stop giggling at anything anyone says at the moment, including Anthony. And he's not *that* funny.

Actually, everyone except Anthony – who didn't have more than a single mimosa – is borderline drunk when our steaming plates finally show up. I plow through my crab cakes like I don't know when my next meal will be.

Even while I'm stuffing my face, I can feel the pull of my phone on my thoughts.

It could be another message.

Or another match.

My fork clatters off my empty plate when I set it down.

My nerves are too bad for me to be this drunk.

The laughter around me is growing in volume and my head is starting to spin, just a little. Headache should arrive at any moment… "Hey, do you need to get that?"

It feels as if the contents of my head slosh against my skull when I turn to look at Anthony on my right.

He gestures toward my purse. "That's a pretty loud notification."

Is it? I cock my head at him. He must be the only one present who is not in his cups at the moment. How boring.

And why is he all in my business?

I don't even know why I was stressing so much over whether or not this man was a good match for me; this outing has revealed to me everything I need to know. I already don't fit into the teeny, tidy box he has ready for whatever wife he chooses to claim.

I need a man who knows out of the gate I don't fit into anyone's box, and I don't think I'm going to find him at Mount Vernon Missionary Baptist Church.

Fuck it – I'm checking my phone right now.

"Hey, y'all excuse me for a second – gotta run to the bathroom really quick."

The ladies are on at least their third round of mimosas and wave me off, their laughter having turned into outright cackling that is drawing the attention of the better-behaved patrons of the restaurant.

Rather than lurking behind the public restroom door, this time I retreat to the safety and privacy of an actual stall.

After all the alcoholic liquid sunshine I consumed, using the toilet is an absolute necessity, but I fumble around with my phone before I leave to wash my hands.

My entire body is trembling as I open the app. I see a new message in my inbox and tap with my finger to open it.

It's the mysterious "J" again.

Gorgeous — I guess that'll be your new name, since there's no chance the one on your profile is legit. That's okay; keep your secrets. It'll be fun to guess.

- J

That little compliment sends my heart racing. "J" is a witty one, but I wonder then if his profile will measure up to the image of the stud he's building up to be in my head.

I'm nervous at what I'll see, afraid of the disappointment that'll come crashing down upon me after what transpired — or rather, what didn't — today with Anthony.

I tap his profile and wait a moment for it to load.

Holy baby Jesus.

What I see is a Greek god of a man, a rock-solid Adonis carved into honey brown granite for the sole purpose of my enjoyment. I read through his bio word for word. Even that's sexy. He speaks of living in the moment and the supreme enjoyment of taking things to the very edge… in an instant, I can see his hands all over me in my burning thoughts, wrapping around my throat and squeezing…

I have to swallow to stop salivating.

This delicious man wants me to talk to him. And fulfill my darkest fantasies, according to his bio.

I want to send him a message so badly, but I've never felt more afraid than I do right now.

Should I be witty or coy? Act shy and reserved? I wouldn't be inauthentic; I can be all of those things at one point or another.

In my drunken state, I don't know what to say without sounding like a hooker trying to get a date.

I can feel myself deflate a bit at the thought that my opening the door to this world will lead to nothing but destruction.

No, I need to think about this. Take my time so I don't say something dumb and regretful.

The floor feels like it's moving under my feet as I exit the stall with my purse and head to the sink to soap up my hands. I really shouldn't have had so much champagne.

I'm unsteady on my feet as I walk back to our table to find everyone gossiping, trying to guess which deacon is allegedly having an affair with the choir director.

I catch Sherry's attention when I return to my seat.

"Hey, I wanted to get your opinion on something."

Sherry's eyes are glassy but she's still coherent. Her ears practically perk up. "What's up, girl?"

Tread carefully, Brooklyn.

"So, I have this friend that I work with that has been dealing with this problem that's she not sure how to deal with."

Sherry's lips purse. "What kind of problem? A man problem?" I consider this, then say, "Man-adjacent."

"Okay," Sherry says on a laugh.

I lean closer so I can speak into her ear. "She told me she recently discovered she likes… freakier activities in bed than she used to."

Sherry leans forward, instantly at full engagement in the conversation. "Is that right? Like what?"

God, I so appreciate that she doesn't appear to think I'm referring to myself in actuality. "That she likes, well… *pain* in the bedroom department. Or really, that she needs it to…" My hand makes a vague gesture while I search for the right words. "…to get over the finish line, if you get what I'm saying."

"Ohhhh, I gotcha." Sherry's drunken whisper is as loud as her regular speaking voice.

"So, what do you think?" My heart hovers in my throat. "Should I tell her she's a freak and move on? She doesn't know what to do."

"Definitely," Sherry says with such conviction my heartbeat stutters in surprise. "Sex and pain don't go together. That shit is weird."

It's a struggle to keep my nonchalant smirk in place. "So, what should I tell her?

"Tell her to keep that freaky nonsense under wraps, but between you and me, your girl has problems."

She does, indeed.

Suddenly, all the sexy energy that had pulsed through me in the restroom leaves my body all at once. That's confirmation if I ever heard it.

Your girl has problems.

Don't I know it. If I go ahead and get rid of the app, never try to explore this new aspect of myself, I'll be safe from my own darkness. I'm not sure anymore if it's worth the risk.

Everyone but Anthony is sloshed by the time we pay our bill and leave, the other ladies supporting each other through their stumbles and laughing hysterically as they make for the door.

I'm not gone quite that far, but Anthony is still gallant enough to help me out of my seat. He literally holds me up when I trip over the threshold onto the sidewalk.

Anthony presses my body against his to keep me from falling and our eyes meet. His are clear and curious as they stare into mine. I can feel his heat through the fabric of his suit and my dress and I still feel *nothing.*

It's simply not there and that makes me sad.

Our group says its goodbye at the next major intersection and we begin to part ways. I hug Sherry tightly and push her and Katrina into a cab to ensure they get home safely. Paulette heads off to crash for the rest of the afternoon at a cousin's apartment, and I'm left standing with Anthony.

"Are you taking a cab, too?" he asks.

I shake my head. "No, I'm gonna walk. I can use the fresh air at the moment."

"Then you should let me walk with you, then – "

"No, that's okay," I say, cutting him off before he can get all of his proverbial shining armor on. "It's broad daylight and I'm a big girl. I can handle myself."

"Then at least take my number in case you need anything."

He holds out a hand to patiently wait for my phone. I make a face – *so pushy.*

And I couldn't say why if I tried, but I dig my cell out of my purse and plop it unlocked into his palm.

He taps in his number and hands it right back.

I hold up the phone in an awkward salute. "Thanks."

"Be careful, Brooklyn." Anthony eyes me thoughtfully as he edges away. "And I'm always available if you ever… need someone to talk to."

I don't know what to say to that, so I nod and give him a big wave until he disappears into the crowd.

Alone again, I turn and face the opposite direction. Now the sun is way too bright and the pigeons are way too loud. Everything stinks and the food I ate tastes like sawdust on the back of my tongue.

Sherry said it. I have problems. It doesn't matter how many other people around the world are into what I'm into. They aren't here with me, in my social circles, living my life. It's just me.

The closer I get to my block, the glummer I feel. So much so that I make a hard right to raid my favorite bodega. Only white chocolate raspberry ice cream can make this right, at least for the moment.

My feet drag for so long, the streetlights are on and the night doorman is on his post when I make it back to my apartment.

"Hey, Fred," I say as I pass on my way to the bank of elevators. He gives a wave in my peripheral, but I'm already concentrating on my ice cream like it holds the meaning of life.

I keep eating spoonful after decadent spoonful as I enter my apartment, even through shedding my clothes in my bedroom and leaving them where they lay, wriggling into a pair of sweats and a raggedy Biggie Smalls t-shirt. I have no sexy left after the emotional rollercoaster I've been on all day.

When I curl up in the corner of my couch, I don't bother turning on the TV. I eat and stare into space and wonder for the thousandth time how I ended up this way.

Eric would say my neuroses are showing. The thought makes me sneer at myself. It's not very late… I'll bet he's up.

I pull up his contact info on my phone and wait.

He picks up on the fourth ring, like always. "Hey, Brook."

I can feel my shoulder muscles relax and I smile into the partial darkness of my living room. "I need your thoughts. Are you busy?"

"Never too busy for you."

My chest warms. I'm glad that he and I discovered we were much better friends than lovers all those years ago.

"Besides," Eric says, "I just finished working out and needed a break anyway."

I snort. "Of course, you did. I feel like you say that every time I talk to you."

His rumbling laughter reminds me of days gone by in a sweet, nostalgic kind of way.

"What can I say? I work out a lot."

I hear shuffling on the other end of the line, like he's lying down somewhere and trying to get comfortable. "So, what's up?"

I release a slow sigh, not sure where to start. Clearing my throat, I steel myself.

"Say you have a friend that you've known a long time, right?" A pause.

"Okay…"

"And you learn something about this friend that may or may not be disturbing to you."

"Like what?"

"Like… she-they like to be hurt during sex. Like, actual pain, not just a little bit of playful spanking."

Eric is quiet so long I feel a flash of panic. "Are you there?"

"Yeah, I'm here. So, what are you asking?"

Isn't it obvious?

"Would you feel differently about this friend?"

"Why would I? People like what they like; it's got nothing to do with me or our 'friendship'."

I almost sigh with relief but catch myself at the last second.

"Okay. And what would you tell your friend if they asked you for advice about their… situation? If they were trying to decide whether or not they should explore this new part of their sexuality?"

Eric laughs. "You sound like a brochure."

I chuckle. "Shut up. Just answer the question."

"The only thing I would tell them," Eric says, "is to do what they feel but only if they are as safe about it as they possibly can be. No unnecessary risks."

Nodding despite the fact that my old friend can't see me, I say quietly, "That makes sense."

We fall into a comfortable silence for a moment, one borne of the many years since our freshman year of college that cemented our platonic bond.

"Just be safe about it, Brooklyn," Eric says, all the mirth gone from his voice.

I give a sad little giggle. Should have known he'd realize I was talking about myself eventually.

"I will; don't worry."

"I always worry. You tend to be reckless, in case you forgot."

That triggers a hearty belly laugh that I feel down to my toes. "Not in many years, friend."

"Yeah, that's what you say," Eric says, laughing in that loud and easy way of his. "Listen, I gotta cut out. Wife's got dinner on the stove and I promised her I'd eat with her tonight."

That vague dull ache beneath my sternum returns as it always does at the mention of someone I care about with a family. Not in jealously because I want to be with Eric, but because part of me still wants what he has with his wife so badly.

"Go, enjoy your dinner. I'm sure it'll be delicious. Thank you, Eric."

"No worries, Brook."

Once we hang up, I feel a tiny sense of hope along with the usual emptiness. I wonder if it's enough to give me courage.

Switching to the BDSM app, I pull up the message from "J" and stare at it for a long time.

I can still delete the app and go back to life as normal, save with tortuously erotic dreams that lead to no chance of fulfillment.

Or, I can take charge of my own destiny and see where this path leads me, for better or worse.

When I really stop and consider, the choice is clear.

Hi J.,

Your profile photo isn't bad either. It's so nice, in fact, that I'll even give you three guesses at my name.

Let's see how you do.

- B

Three

I don't hear back from my digital pen pal right away, so I go ahead and get on with my nighttime routine – a salad with chicken for dinner, some rachet TV while I eat it, a nice hot shower when I'm done and then crawling into crisp, clean sheets.

I plug my phone in on the nightstand charger and stare at it in the dark for a full half-hour before I give up.

He doesn't reply all night, but it's fine. J's profile photo alone is more than enough to trigger the fantasies that bring me to the brink by my own hand twice before I finally pass out in bed.

As usual, I don't stay asleep long and spend the remainder of the night gazing at the ceiling.

My hand is reaching for my phone the next morning before my alarm ever goes off.

I'm back on the app in seconds and feel my heart sink.

No response to my message and no new messages.

It's still fine. I'm not going to get upset over something so frivolous. I'm a busy, adult woman with obligations and important things to do.

I jump out of bed, leaving my phone on the mattress as I get ready for work. The screen is facing up so I can see it from the bathroom. And the walk-in closet. And the sitting area.

There are still no notifications by the time I'm in my suit and heels. *Shit.*

Okay, okay. I need to stop this before my compulsion gets out of hand when it comes to that app. It's already making me insane with anticipation.

I make a point to throw my cell into my purse when I head to the kitchen to throw breakfast together. I eat standing up at the counter, shooting daggers at my purse.

Why hasn't he responded yet? Maybe I came off too aloof. My response probably needed to be sexier or wittier.

I huff. This is stupid.

Snatching up my purse and briefcase, I lock up and make my way to the subway station down the block and try to ignore the fact that it feels like I'm waiting for a dirty bomb in my bag to go off.

"Hola, Enrique," I call to the cashier at my bodega as he rings up my coffee and Danish.

"Hola, chica!" He flashes me a toothy grin and says something to me in a flurry of Spanish. I only catch every other word.

"You know I'm not fluent yet…and I'm still not having your baby, if that's what you said."

Enrique understands English well enough and laughs as he sends me off with my brown paper bag and coffee.

I find an empty seat on the train and settle in for the ride to the station, munching on my warmed pastry – thanks again, Enrique – and sipping the coffee that I sit in the empty seat next to me. All the while I pointedly ignore the very concept of extracting my phone from my closed purse and doing what I want to do more now than I ever have before.

After the next three stops, I convince myself that J, whoever he is, has already moved on. After all, we're all anonymous strangers on the app. I'm no one to him and vice versa. He owes me nothing. I'm losing my mind over less than three sentences.

All those thoughts evaporate when my notifications ring and I nearly jump out of my skin, earning concerned looks from other passengers nearby.

If I was tired from my insomnia before, I'm fully alert now.

In fact, I'm on what feels like the verge of a panic attack as I open the app once again and check my inbox messages.

What an interesting proposition, Gorgeous. I like the way you think already.

Let's see… Brittany seems too mundane to be worthy of you, so I'm going to ride with Bianca. Am I close?

-J

It takes an act of sheer will to keep myself from squealing like a teen girl- child right there on the train. Oh, my God!

I take a deep breath to get a grip and stop hyperventilating.

Part of me thinks I should keep him waiting as long as he had me on pins and needles. The other part simply can't wait another moment.

J,

Strong effort. A good guess, but still way off the mark. Think less bourgeoisie and more street.

- B

My heart races for the next three stops as I wait with bated breath for his reply.

I nearly drop my coffee when the next message comes through.

Hmm, I sense this is a test I don't want to fail with you… give me some time to think on it.

-J

I catch my bottom lip in my teeth to smother my smile. This should not make me this happy, and yet…

When I really think about it, this is the first time in a long time I feel like I truly have something new and unpredictable to look forward to.

I'm floating on clouds when I reach my office, exactly on time instead of early as I normally am since the train was late.

My assistant, Nikki, is already waiting for me in my office. She trades me a fresh cup of coffee for my briefcase and puts it away under lock and key.

"You look nice," I say, eyeing her oxblood pencil skirt, black blouse and stilettos. Seems she took my advice when I told her she needed to dress for the job she wants. Hopefully she's not ready to try for mine just yet.

She smiles but she's already on the move again. "Thanks! But you have no time to sit down… you have a meeting in ten minutes.

Crap… with everything going on, I forgot all about it. "Okay, I'll be there."

She nods and rushes the folder tucked into her arms and filled with papers to my desk. "There's everything you need for the meeting."

I call out my thanks after her, but she's already back on the move. That girl never stops moving.

When I reach into my purse for my compact to touch up my makeup, my hand hesitates, knowing my phone is so close by…

No, I can't take it into a meeting. That's beyond irresponsible, if not outright rude.

Isn't it?

I check my watch and realize I only have a minute or two to spare.

I'll put my phone on silent.

I flick the switch on the side and it vibrates once to confirm that mode is activated. Then I slide my feet back into the heels I kicked off and hightail it to the conference room with my coffee.

The other producers are here, and as I look around the room, I realize we are the only women in attendance. I sit down next to Debbie Penn, the producer who trained me and the person who taught me the game when it came to women in this cutthroat industry.

The most important lesson I learned from her was that you will always have to make yourself be seen.

I feel seen right now, but in a way that has nothing to do with office politics. If someone were to ask me after this meeting what it was about, I'd have no idea what to say. My eyes are glued to the cell phone I keep balanced on my thigh under the huge conference room table.

Okay. I don't want to make any assumptions, but I thought I'd try something with a little more "color"....Briseida?

-J

My sudden snort of laughter catches the attention of everyone at the table as one of the junior producers is going over pitches the network received from an outside production company.

"Sorry — allergies," I say, sniffling and ducking my head to conveniently look at my lap again.

I glance up every so often so it's not painfully obvious I'm typing on my phone.

J,

I appreciate your respect for diversity, but this guess is even further off the mark. One more try for a treat.

- B

In my excitement, I hit send before I've fully processed my reply. Damn, that may have been a little too suggestive this early on in the conversation.

"Brooklyn, did you have anything to add?"

Debbie nudges my ankle under the table.

"Not today," I say to the room with a broad smile as I raise my head, not missing a beat. One of the perks of being a boss is no one questioning you when you're clearly too distracted to function in a meeting.

Something about this just feels right in my gut: Brooke.
Did I nail it?

- J

He's so close it's a little scary, and I don't know if I should still be excited or concerned that I may have accidently typed my real name in on the app somewhere. But I double check and there's nothing obvious that gave me away.

J,

You're so close, I'll let you go ahead and use that name.
Are you ever going to tell me yours? Fair is fair.

- B

I can hear the low drone of multiple voices all around me, so I'm sure the meeting is still going on. Regardless, I can't tear my focus away from my phone screen while I wait for his reply.

Parched, I sip from a glass of water placed on the table by the office secretary.

Oh Brooke,

J can be a name in itself as much as it is an initial. Regardless, it's the only name you'll be screaming once I get ahold of you — if you allow such a supreme pleasure, of course.

- J

The photo he attached shows his naked muscled body all the way down to the root of what looks to be a *very* substantial piece of meat and instantly ignites my imagination. I choke on a mouthful of water in my shock at his response, launching myself into an intense coughing fit that forces me to make a run for the restroom with my face aflame.

As soon as I feel like I can breathe normally again, I type him a hurried message:

J,

Haven't you heard of NSFW labels? Your photo nearly got me fired. Not that it wouldn't have been worth it for the peek…

Brooke

I pace the restroom for the thirty seconds it takes for him to answer me.

Brooke,

If that's the case, I can only imagine how I can make you squirm with my voice in your ear.

- J

I can't believe this is happening. A man – a beautiful man – who can actually string together coherent sentences in English is having a full-blown flirty conversation with me at this moment. He's barely said anything risqué but the flood in my panties is back in full effect.

And he wants to talk to me. Today, on the phone. Probably right now.

I… I'm not sure what to say yet, so I temporarily tuck my phone into the front pocket of my suit pants and walk back toward the conference room. I can see through the glass wall that it's now empty except for Debbie. When she sees me, she rolls her eyes playfully and waves me off.

I take that as a green light to go back to my office. Nikki has already left a folder labeled "meeting minutes" on my desk, God bless her.

Plopping back into my chair, I pull out my phone yet again like a teenager and realize I've missed a silent message notification since my restroom break.

Brooke,

I know I can make you a believer if you want to give me a call. The next step is up to you.

- J

He gave me his phone number, right there in black and white. Well, this escalated quickly, but I'm not uncomfortable with it. Not in the slightest, but things are heating up fast enough to be volatile and I still have to do *some* work today.

I force myself to focus on my job for the rest of the morning until I can't take it anymore and announce that I'm taking off early.

I'm back on the subway by midafternoon, staring at the number I've keyed into my phone. I haven't hit the call button yet. It's going to make all of this real and I'm… not sure I'm ready yet.

Still, I did say I would need courage to handle this, and courage cannot exist without the presence of fear.

Taking a deep breath, I call him before I change my mind.

It rings twice before he picks up.

"Hello?"

My heart bangs once, then twice against my ribs.

After a moment, my mouth remembers how to speak. "J, I take it?"

His resonant chuckle literally makes my toes curl.

"Ah yes, Gorgeous Brooke… how are you?"

I must control the giggling.

"I can say I'm a lot better now than I was earlier this morning." How strange is it that I feel like this is not the first conversation we've had? I don't recognize his voice at all, but there's a certain quality to it that feels eerily familiar. I notice I'm licking my lips and I have to force myself to stop.

"Likewise." He pauses as if listening. "You going somewhere? You sound like you're outside."

"I'm on the train on my way home."

"In the middle of the day?" He sounds pleased, like he knows why. "I took off early."

His satisfied laugh reminds me of deep, dark chocolate. "You went through all that trouble just for me?"

"A happy accident," I say with a smile.

The rest of the way home, he surprises me by keeping our exchange light, like two strangers chatting in line at the grocery store. We both complain about the unseasonably warm weather and get into a lively debate regarding the complexities of coffee, the drink of choice for each of us, if he is to be believed.

I'm feeling as if I'm having an overdue check-in with an old friend by the time I get home and kick off my heels.

"Now it sounds like you made it home."

"I did," I say, tossing my stuff in a chair and sinking myself down onto the couch with a sigh of relief.

"Good. There's something I want you to try for me, but only if you feel comfortable enough to trust me."

"What do you mean?" Alarm bells sound off in my head as I wait for him to explain.

"How do you feel physically when you talk to me? Describe it."

An odd question, but I indulge him as I curl my feet under me on the couch.

"I feel… warm. Relaxed. Comfortable, probably more than I should be."

"Do you feel comfortable enough to get out of your clothes right now?"

Hell, I'm halfway there already.

God, that *voice…* in my heightened state as of this morning, I'm willing to do just about anything at this point to get some satisfaction.

Standing up, I quickly pull off my work clothes and leave them in a pile on the end of the couch, panties and all.

This is so crazy. Seriously crazy, but I can't stop myself from bending to his will.

I sit back down on the couch. "Done," I tell him.

"Good," J says, and the way he said it makes my core clench hard. "Are you sitting down?"

"Yes." My trembling voice comes out like a croak.

"Now take both of your hands and stroke your skin. I want you to pretend they're mine."

Oh, God.

Just as in my fantasies, I move my hands over my body as if they belonged to him while J whispers increasingly naughty instructions in my ear.

My arousal jumps into the stratosphere so quickly I don't have time to feel shame. I just have this need that demands to be fulfilled.

In minutes, J has me tweaking my breasts to intense peaks that only heighten the pleasurable pressure. My legs can't keep still. I'm half afraid he can hear my pulsing heartbeat over my labored breathing into the phone.

"That's it, gorgeous." He's coaxing me closer and closer to something I have no name for, something huge and wonderful and terrifying.

When he has me sink three hooked fingers into my body instead of my usual two, I'm nearly at the brink.

"Work those hips, babe." J blows into the phone, and I distantly wonder if he's doing something similar where he is.

"I know how much you need it. I could hear it in your voice."

I whimper, working myself against my fingers faster.

"Tell me," J says, his voice now a low growl, "are you close?"

Intense. It's too intense. My head rocks from side to side. What's coming is a monster with which I am completely unfamiliar and I'm almost afraid.

"Yes," I say, no longer recognizing the guttural voice or the woman it's supposed to be attached to.

He tells me his intention and I give in to his soft-spoken demand with a ferocious blush, taking my other hand and landing smack after hard smack across my mound. The sharp, sudden movement jars the thick bulb of flesh between my lips, more engorged than I have ever seen it.

I cry out with each impact, pumping so furiously with my other hand that I've broken a sweat.

J groans. "You're so beautiful, Brooke… smack it as hard as you can and think of me when you cum…"

And I do. The pain on my most sensitive flesh would have made any other woman hit the roof in agony, but J's guidance made my final solid smack the perfect balance of ecstatic pleasure and pain… I scream so loud I'm sure the neighborhoods heard the thunderous orgasm roaring down on me and sucking out my soul. I whine and whine, hips jerking as I ride out one wave of blistering ecstasy after another.

It takes me forever to come down. When I do, J is still there, whispering words of praise in my ear for how good I did, of how beautiful I sounded to him.

This, by far, is the most twisted thing I've ever done. I'm still sopping wet and ready to do it again.

When I can finally catch my breath, I make my feelings known, heedless of how crazy I sound.

"When did you want to meet in person?"

Four

As they say, all good things must come to an end.

Despite the fact that I have never in my life produced an orgasm so intense that it takes a full minute to remember my own name, the spine-tingling euphoria finally begins to fade in my body like a sunset over Central Park.

My chest gradually stops heaving. My desperate panting against the quiet of my apartment lessens. The quieter I become, the louder the silence around me becomes.

The more my heartbeat begins to normalize, the hotter my face burns with shame.

Jesus, what have I done?

I realize then I can still hear J breathing heavily in my ear from where I still have my phone pressed painfully against my cheekbone. I loosen my death grip on the device with a wince. I probably left a mark.

The man on my phone gives a soft groan and I hear what sounds like the faint rustle of sheets. A man who still is, in nearly every way, a stranger.

J… if that's even his real name.

God, of course it isn't – *it's a fucking initial.* I know nothing about him, and here I am sharing intimacies with nothing more substantive than a masculine voice dripping with poisoned honey, his words echoing in my head when I reached the peak of ecstasy like my thoughts were made of him and him alone.

I never knew I could go there. I never knew there was a *there* to go to.

A deep, full-body shudder makes my sweaty skin erupt in goosebumps.

If this whole… interlude wasn't proof there is something twisted happening in my head, I don't know what is…

I press my lips together and snap my knees closed, wincing a little at the throbbing echo my wet fingers have left behind deep in my center. I'm actually a little tender. I've never been that rough with myself before.

"Gorgeous… you still with me?"

I'm too busy scrambling for the throw on the back of the couch to cover myself with to answer at first. Once I have the silky chenille blanket tucked tightly around my nakedness, I retreat to the corner of the couch. I resist covering my head with the blanket like a child. Barely.

I take the deepest possible breath I can without it being audible and let it out in a long, silent *whoosh.*

"I'm here," I finally say, barely recognizing the raw croak of my own voice.

"Good. I was worried you had disappeared on me."

Oh, I'm contemplating it. But ghosting a sexy man post-phone sex does not make for very adult-like behavior. Am I or am I not a grown woman?

No, I'm going to be mature about this – but what I will *not* do is beg to see him when I know good and well this conversation of ours needs to be the last one. This can't be healthy for me. And frankly, I'm not used to looking this thirsty to any man, let alone one I haven't even seen in the flesh.

Clearing my throat, I try my damndest to recover the sense of feminine pride I'd cast aside the moment I threw my legs open at J's whispered command.

"So. That was… interesting."

J chuckles at my brevity and I try – really, really hard – to ignore the fresh shivers he makes dance up and down and back up my spine.

"That's one way to put it."

He's quiet for half a second and I start to panic. What if it's awkward now? What am I supposed to say after busting it open for him – albeit virtually – and giving him firsthand knowledge of the noises that I make when I come?

My chest gets tight, like my lungs became a size too small when I wasn't paying attention. I slap a hand atop my sternum and try to force myself to breathe normally. My eyes go wide when I feel that same hand trembling.

Am I about to have a panic attack or something?

Maybe I jumped the gun a little when I said I wanted to see him. I can't even govern myself appropriately while interacting with him in the privacy of my own apartment. It's too soon.

It's way too soon.

"If you think it's too soon, we don't have to rush anything, you know."

Shit – I said that out loud?

Goddamit…

I'm not even sure how it's possible, but I feel the heat pooling in my cheeks go from uncomfortably warm to lava-like in an instant. "I mean… I wouldn't want to make you uncomfortable," I manage to say, swallowing convulsively in my suddenly dry throat. Clearly, *I'm* the one uncomfortable, but maybe he can't hear it in my voice.

"I'm not uncomfortable at all," J says in a low purr, "but I would like to know how you're feeling at this moment. About what you just experienced."

I gnaw my bottom lip. How am I supposed to answer that?

I feel confused, embarrassed, and slightly nauseous at the wanton way I reveled in this new and terrifying aspect of my personality. Mostly, I'm afraid – afraid of the future implications of my having enjoyed it so much.

"You can be honest with me," J says.

I hold the phone more tightly against my ear. I can hear J's soft breathing on the other line, steady and consistent. Unrattled. Unbothered. He doesn't rush me to speak or explain. He waits with the kind of patience I've only seen exhibited by nuns and old men playing chess in the park.

When I hear that chuckle again, it makes me crack a smile of my own.

"Let me make it easier for you: have you ever done anything like that before?"

The urge to lie comes on so strong, I can taste its bitterness on the back of my tongue. But I resist. There is a tiny part of me that wants to see where this goes, and I don't want to build upon a holey foundation made of dishonesty.

It doesn't make sense, and it's likely to come back and bite me in the ass, but there's still something about J that feels safe.

"I think you already know the answer to that," I say instead, rolling my eyes at him and at myself.

"That may be, but I want to hear you say it."

Sigh.

"No, I have never done anything like that before in my life."

"So… you've never touched your pussy before?"

My mouth opens to protest just before I realize he's making a joke.

Oh, har har.

"Of course, I have. Just…" – I shift on the couch, my skin suddenly hot and prickly all over – "…not like *that*."

I hear shifting again, like J's trying to get more comfortable. A vision of him based upon his app profile photo dances before my mind's eye, J's rippling abs on full display as he reclines on his bed with pure white sheets rumpled all around him and pure devilment in his eyes –

"Hey, did you hear me?"

I start, blinking out of my impromptu fantasy. "Sorry, what?"

"I was wondering if it's safe to assume you also have never come like that. It almost sounded like you were being skinned alive."

Ugh, if it was that bad, I *know* my neighbors had to have heard. I'm surprised security didn't come knocking at my door for a welfare check.

Sorry guys, I would have said, *nothing to see here but a single woman engaging in a little kinky, semi-anonymous phone sex. Move along.*

I realize I'm blushing again. Furiously. "God – can we not talk about my noises – "

"You have nothing to be ashamed of."

Hearing no evidence of jest in J's voice, another smile sneaks up on me. His earnestness keeps taking me off guard. Here I am thinking that this was all about sex and this guy takes it upon himself to chip away at some of the shame I'm feeling about this entire situation as a whole in addition to my behavior tonight.

I tuck a loose strand of hair behind my ear and duck my head. "Ah, thanks for that."

Nibbling on my lip again, I contemplate his previous question. "I guess…" I pause, searching for the words, "…I guess on some level I do feel a sense of freedom, I guess?"

I cringe, wishing I didn't phrase it like it question. I sound like a dopey teenager. Clearing my throat, I continue, trying to be as open as I can.

"I've never felt quite that high before. Something about the way the pleasure and the pain mixing in equal amounts right at the perfect moment…" My eyes slip closed, remembering the heights I'd scaled with J in my ear. "It was on another level."

J hummed his agreement and it gave me the courage to keep going.

"I've had lovers in the past that I thought were amazing, and I've even had pretty good sessions alone, but I have *never* come that hard in my life."

"It's beautiful, isn't it?" That low, knowing purr of his is back. This time I literally let myself relax into it, my head falling back against the couch.

"When you add pain to the mix," J says, "it twists around the pleasure like barbed wire and intensifies it in a way that can't otherwise be achieved. Gorgeous and otherworldly, exactly like you."

I preen at the compliment, my fingertips skimming the exposed skin of my collarbone.

"I bet you say that to all the girls." A giggle bubbles out of me. "Is pain… something you've always been into?"

J pauses so long, I worry that I've already put my foot in my mouth and overstepped.

I hurriedly open my mouth to smooth things over with some kind of joke, but to my utter relief, J is already speaking again.

"There was a woman I met when I was younger who introduced me to the concept, and then the lifestyle."

Hm… who was this woman to him? His description suggested their relationship was a long time ago, but I can still hear the fondness in his voice.

I make a face at the pang of jealousy I feel. "Did you like it immediately, or was it something you had to develop a taste for it? Like caviar, or something."

J laughs. "Once you know you can come with your balls clamped in a vice, there's no going back."

This time it's me who bursts out laughing, and I laugh so long and hard that I snort and have to slap a hand over my mouth. I can hear him laughing with me over the phone and try to apologize between gasps and wheezes. I don't want him to think I'm making fun at his expense.

I don't get that impression when J tells me it's okay, still snickering. "Your reaction is actually rather refreshing. It's an excellent reminder that good sex is supposed to be fun, even if it can sometimes be a little… dark."

"What's your favorite aspect of 'the lifestyle', as you put it?" Whatever it is, I want to try it. Maybe.

"Oh, babygirl… there are far too many dark and delicious things I have explored for me to be able to pick just one," J says. "Although I will say, hearing how beautiful you sound when you come has become a highlight."

A full grin stretches across my face at that. "Well, I definitely feel less embarrassed about it now."

"Good. You should never be ashamed of your pleasure."

I may need to hold him to that.

This time, the moment of silence that slips in between us is comfortable and warm instead of tense and fraught with uncertainty.

J speaks again first. "I don't think I have ever been this open with someone I just met before, especially not someone I haven't seen in person."

"Really?" The center of my chest warms. Is this special to him?

Am *I*?

"Yes. I'm not usually this open with new people, let alone a woman I'm interested in."

"And you're 'interested' in me, I take it?" I deeply desire to hear him say it.

Something tells me if J were standing in front of me right now, he'd be smirking. "I think you already know the answer to that question," he says, echoing my snark from earlier in the conversation. Well-played.

"That said," he continues, "if you really do feel comfortable enough to meet in person, let me know and I'll be there. But we don't have to do anything you don't want to do."

His statement removes the remaining pressure. What do I really want? What would I do if I had no fear of judgement burning within myself?

"I know I would very much like to get to know you better, J. Much better."

"And if we could get together… tomorrow, would you want to?"

It's time for me to start letting go of the fear.

I take a deep breath and a leap of faith. "Yeah. Yeah, I would." J mirrors my breath. "I would, too. If I could."

"What do you mean?"

"I have to go out of town for work for the next week."

The heaviness of the disappointment that settles over me is shocking. "Oh." I try not to pout and fail miserably.

"But we can hook up when I get back – I mean, get together. If you still want to." Hearing him suffer from a bit of foot-in-mouth-disease himself puts me more at ease. If there's a chance my mystery man is as affected by all this as I am…

"I think there's a good chance I will."

"Good." It makes me happy to be able to hear the smile in his voice and it triggers yet another of my own. "I'll hit you up the second I get back. I promise."

I have never looked forward to something more. My entire body is trembling with nervous energy. It takes a great deal of effort to sound like I'm not ready to run naked through my apartment in excitement.

"Sounds good to me."

From the moment I sign off with J, he invades my mind like some kind of sexy virus, taking over each one of my thoughts the second they are formed.

Distracted is not the word for how I drift through the next couple of days. I move like a zombie, dependent upon routine alone to float me through each morning, afternoon, and evening.

Wake up, breakfast, train, work.

Meetings, phone calls, lunch, more meetings, train.

Pick up dinner, walk home, eat, watch a documentary, take a bath, get in bed, dream of the voice I have not been able to stop thinking about, no matter how hard I try.

More than once when I lay alone under my sheets, staring up at the dark ceiling for hours, my hand drifts across my breasts and down my stomach before I realize the intention of my sexually frustrated subconscious. Every time, I snatch my hand back before it can bury itself between my thighs.

I know whatever I do to myself won't satisfy. Not after what I experienced with J over the phone. It's crazy, but I almost feel like trying to rub one out without him in my ear would be akin to being unfaithful, which is absolutely absurd. But it's as if my pussy already knows it belongs to J before either of us has set eyes on him.

The desire that had been relegated to background static in my day-to-day life has repositioned itself front and center. Now it feels more like a banked fire licking through my veins at all times. I'm lucky if I get an hour or two of sleep every night. The ache deep inside my core is so bad it's nearly painful, and it has only gotten worse since J went out of town.

My experience with him was like expecting to pop your regular aspirin for a constant headache and having someone slip you a tiny hit of heroin instead.

That orgasm blew my head off. I can still feel slight echoes of it in my body days later and the craving for another is becoming unbearable. I've only had a taste and now I want – need – more.

So. Much. More.

J seems to have turned me into an orgasm fiend overnight. Or maybe I'm already a fiend for the man himself.

Only time will tell. As it is, the week he'll be away can't go by fast enough.

At first, I think work will keep me too busy to obsess about J's promise to contact me when he returns, but I quickly learn that's a pipe dream. Any free moment that presents itself finds me with phone in hand, compulsively checking for missed texts or calls and trying to will J's number to flash across the screen.

This is ridiculous.

"Boss, are you okay?"

At work, I look up to find my assistant staring at me, her head poked into the doorway of my office from the hallway.

"Sorry, Nikki… what's up?"

"I've been knocking for like, five minutes."

See? This is what I'm talking about. What happened to me? I talk to J once and now I'm useless.

With a sigh, I smooth my hands over my loose chignon and sit back in my high-backed chair, shoulders slumped in defeat.

Nikki shakes her head and walks over to perch on the corner of my desk. "What's going on with you?" The genuine concern etched into the soft contours of my loyal assistant's face makes my gut twist with real guilt. She works so hard and all I seem to do lately is waste everybody's time, including my own, indulging girlish fantasies. "You've barely said two words to me or anyone the last couple of days, and no amount of concealer would ever cover up dark circles that bad."

I wince. Nikki isn't pulling any punches this morning. But she's right.

"I haven't really been sleeping," I say, passing a hand over my tired eyes.

Nikki purses her red lips in thought for a moment. "When's the last time you took an actual day off?"

It sounds so foreign spoken aloud, I blink at her in complete befuddlement. I have always enjoyed my work, so taking off never held much promise of pleasure for me. At the moment, however, my thoughts are all over the place and I want to be anywhere but here.

"You know, I honestly can't remember."

Nikki snorts, already heading for the door. She tosses her flippant command over her shoulder before she leaves. "Go home, boss."

Well, I literally can't get any work done and my assistant has effectively dismissed me. So, before I can embarrass myself and tarnish my corporate reputation, I leave a note on my desk that I'll be out sick for a couple of days before I grab my bag and practically run out of the door.

It's the eve of the weekend, and I've been off work for the last three days. I still don't quite know what to do with myself.

The first thing that crossed my mind when I got home early that first afternoon – obviously – was throwing my silly inhibitions to the wind and blowing the release valve on all that pent-up sexual tension still coiled tightly inside me since the night I talked with J. It seemed so long ago that no amount of rubbing myself with wet fingers could produce even a smidge of the fire J had created in me with his words and smoky tone. Just as I feared. My mental spank bank full of sexy memories had lost all of its juice after J had blown its capacity to bits with a single session.

So, I gave up and just… ached. What else could I do? I know now that I need the real thing and my body would accept no substitutes.

After spending that first day home cleaning my apartment top to bottom with nothing but a toothbrush, a bottle of alcohol and a microfiber rag, I was too tired to leave the place the following day. I didn't call anyone either, content to situate myself in a corner of my couch – opposite the location of the "incident", as I was trying to put it out of my head for the time being – eating fancy takeout from restaurants selling plates at 200+ dollars a pop and watching sappy romcoms from the 90's. This was *my* time.

By the next day, I was sick of it.

Now, I'm out in Manhattan's bustling streets, the late afternoon sun feeling strong and strange across my back. I can't remember the last time I've been free of obligation during this time of day. I take my time meandering, leaning into each minute that passes instead of rushing through them all like I normally do. One could never explore every nuance of the infinite number of streets in the city, but today I find myself wandering with no sense of purpose – watching flocks of grackles twist and turn in the steam belching from the sides of buildings, nibbling on an ice cream cone I buy from a mobile cart and shivering with the slight chill still clinging to the air despite my thick denim jacket.

Something like peace settles over me for the first time in a long while. Maybe all I needed was a few days off after all.

I keep strolling. The breeze changes direction and suddenly smells of fresh French bread. My espresso ice cream is delicious and all is finally right with the world, until a tall and handsome man walking by catches my eye. He doesn't look my way, but the stimuli are enough for my unoccupied mind to regurgitate the images of J burned into my memory – or rather, of his app profile photos. My recently acquired ability to match his voice to the stark male beauty is still doing a number on me.

What would it be like to have him walking through the city next to me, hand in hand?

My God, beyond lame to even *think* that. Still, the raw poignancy of my daydream makes me sadder than I ever expect.

I'm too hopeful; that's what this is. I'm putting all of my love and marriage and relationship eggs in one basket again.

That's dumb and I know it.

It's okay. J said he'd contact me. Maybe he will; maybe he won't. Either way, it's early enough that I can get out relatively unscathed. There's not even anything to get *out* of in the first place.

I *know* this. I do. Imagine my disappointment when J's sexy profile stays affixed in my mind, mocking me with the possibility of a full relationship I'm not even sure I want in the first place.

My eyes find the nearest metal trashcan and I chuck the rest of my ice cream cone. I've lost my taste for something sweet altogether.

I glance at my watch, annoyed with myself. I'm supposed to be at my mom's place in a couple of hours for our weekly family dinner. I'm over taking in the sights and sounds of the neighborhood for the time being, but I can swing by the all-day farmer's market near her house and pick up something to bring since I "forgot" to cook something. I make food for myself all the time; I'm not about to give up any opportunity to let my family feed me. Especially with my mom's cooking.

My mouth waters the entire long walk to the market just thinking about it.

I buy my mom another aloe vera succulent to replace the one she killed (one of many) and stuff it in my purse with its little plastic sack. I'm glad I thought to wear leather flats with my bright floral sundress and didn't try to be too cute in my favorite chunky platform heels; my feet would have been blistered up before I'd made it halfway to my mother's house. Done it enough times in my youth to know better now.

Gotta love wisdom.

My mother's brownstone is situated in the middle of a quiet residential block a few miles south of my apartment on the Upper West Side. It isn't a coincidence that she ended up so close; as her firstborn child, she made a promise to me when I was very young that she would never live more than an hour away so she could always keep an eye on me. When I was a kid, that promise was comforting. By the time I was a teenager and a little older, it was equal parts creepy and annoying. Now, I appreciate to my core that our little family means so much to her that she would pack up her entire life in Pennsylvania a few years ago to move closer to her kids – me, my younger sister and my baby brother.

Carla Samuels opens her front door and gasps when she sees me standing on her stoop.

"Tink!"

I roll my eyes at my mother's use of my ever-embarrassing childhood nickname, but before I can come up with a salty quip, she grabs me into one of her fierce, warm hugs. I immediately feel the tension from the past week begin to melt out of my neck and shoulders. It helps that she smells like French lavender and vanilla sugar. She always smells like she's been baking despite the fact that no one could get her to go anywhere near an oven for that purpose even if you paid her to do it.

"Girl, I wasn't expecting you for hours! What are you doing here so early?"

I'm smiling as hard at her as she is at me when she ushers me inside the foyer. Glossy green plants in terracotta pots have been placed in nearly every corner. The reddish wood floors are immaculately clean. This place is still relatively new to me, but my mother keeps so many framed photos of my siblings and I all over the entry walls and atop the long credenza near the front door – including childhood snaps of me in my sports uniforms for field hockey, basketball and track – that it feels like I could have grown up here in New York.

"I took off work the past couple of days," I say, plopping down onto her comfy overstuffed couch.

Still grinning, my mother steps into a warm shaft of light let in from the front windows and I'm struck all over again by her beauty. Fine, fully defined features, dark chocolate eyes shaped like Jordan almonds. And not the least bit shallow about it. My mother has been busy whipping the city's finest nurses into shape as the nurse supervisor at the largest trauma center in Manhattan; she's seen her share of blood and guts and everything in between, and she has never thought herself too good for the backbreaking work of caring for others.

Carla snorts a laugh and moves through the room to the kitchen, her lithe frame elegant and graceful beneath the voluminous satin of her patterned caftan. "*You?* Taking off work? I don't believe it."

"It's been known to happen from time to time," I say as I leave the couch to follow her, laughing to myself at my own lie. Mom's own laughter rings out at my response; she knows it's a lie, too.

We fall into our usual routine, laughing and talking about nothing, my mother giving my hands a playful slap when I try to sneak peeks into her simmering pots. I know by the heavy scents of garlic and peppers and herbs that it's the makings of something Italian, my favorite. But I pretend not to know what it is so I can keep asking my mother for hints because I know she enjoys it.

And then comes the question that makes the warm family scene crash down around me:

"So, what have you been up to lately, Brooklyn?"

My heart actually stutters, the shame I feel is so sudden and intense. I want to cover my face and hide.

I whip around, grabbing a wooden spoon from the holder on the counter and start stirring the largest pot. Unnecessary, but I can't look my mother in the eye knowing what I did with J over the phone wasn't too far removed from moseying down to the nearest porn store gloryhole and giving some unseen stranger a rub-and-tug.

At least now when she looks at me, she'll think my red face is from the steaming hot food.

"Um, hello? Little girl, I'm talking to you."

She's only half-joking and I still haven't answered her.

"Oh, you know… this and that. I needed to take some time for myself. To… refocus."

She doesn't know the half of it, and it hurts me that I can't bring myself to tell her. I tell my mother everything else about my life, but not whatever this… thing is that I'm doing. I can never tell her about this.

Not for the first time, doubt sifts down around me and blankets the guilt. Why am I so insistent on exploring something that I can only be embarrassed by in front of the people I love and care about?

"Tink, what are you not telling me? What's wrong?"

I keep my back to her and fiddle with the initialed pendant of my delicate gold necklace. After a long moment, Mom's hands ease over my shoulders, as comforting and warm as the woman herself. Tears prick my eyes and I squeeze them shut. It's just frustration. Everything's fine, but I can't cry in front of her. Especially for no real reason.

It's an existential crisis, mother – NBD.

"What are you talking about? I'm fine. Everything is everything." I flash a quick smile at her over my shoulder and spin out of her grasp. "When's the last time you watered your plants?" I find her watering can under the sink, fill it, then dash to the living room.

"You know they can't sprout legs and go get their own water, right?" I'm teasing of course, but she and I both know all twenty of the potted plants placed around her home would be dead as dead could be if I didn't come by and see about them every week. Carla has a black thumb but she could have grown the Garden of Eden with her own hands, if you let her tell it.

Unfortunately for me, Mom follows me. "Are you running because you aren't ready to talk about a man you met?"

I choke on my own saliva. Sometimes I hate that she knows me so well.

"I haven't met a man," I say, looking harder at her potted fern than I need to. I'm terrible at lying, and even though it's technically true since I still haven't seen J in real life, I don't want to risk it.

"Right."

I don't dare look at her behind me.

The doorbell rings and I trap my sigh of relief in my lungs. Salvation in the form of my younger siblings.

Ditching the watering can, I run to the door and squeal when I see my brother and sister like I haven't seen them this past week.

Bianca and Derrick both indulge me tight hugs and kisses and come inside. Four and seven years my junior, respectively, my brother and sister then wriggle out of my hold as quickly as possible and head straight for the kitchen.

It's always this way, my family and me. That happy glow returns as my sister laughs our father's laugh and my brother cracks jokes with our mother's zany humor and I help them all set the table for the four of us.

It's ziti and meat sauce that Mom's made, and it's cheesy and greasy and delicious. Watching my figure for the sake of feeling optimal confidence when I do finally see J flits around in the back of my mind, but I manage to keep it there and eat to my heart's content.

"So, what girl you got chasing you around now, D?" The conversation has turned to our dating lives, and I do my level best to keep the attention off me. I grin at my brother around the cannoli I'm munching on that Bianca picked up from a nearby bakery. It's the second time in the last few minutes that he's avoided my question.

Derrick rolls his eyes, but the smile he wears I know for sure has gotten him whatever he wants time and again. "That'd be *girls plural,* thank you very much."

The hubris of a twenty-something young man.

"Oh, *God.*" Bianca gag-laughs.

"And I'm sure every one of them are young and dumb, like you like 'em," I say.

"At least *somebody* is getting some around here, 'cause it sure ain't *you,* Brook."

Under normal circumstances, I would have thrown my head back and laughed heartily at my loving brother's good-natured jab.

I can't seem to do it today.

Bianca is too busy tossing her hair and gassing up my brother, while he's too busy sucking up her praise to notice the way my face falls before I can catch myself.

But Mom does.

She's noticeably quiet for the rest of dinner, even as the topics we linger over naturally flow in different directions. Once our plates have practically been licked clean, Bianca and Derrick amble off to the living room for the TV, rubbing their overstuffed bellies. I slink off to wash dishes because I don't want to face my family so raw, my sexual deviancy feeling as visible as a brand on my forehead.

"Now I know something's wrong. I don't think you have ever *volunteered* to do dishes."

A sad smile flirts with my lips as I stare into the sink full of fluffy suds and fragrant with eucalyptus and mint. Mom is so extra when it comes to household scents. "I do hate dishes, you know."

"Hey." My mother grabs the hand that's not holding a wet plate. "You want to tell me what happened at the table?"

The words coil on my tongue. I open my mouth to speak… and nothing comes out.

Whatever's happening with me is happening so fast, I can barely keep up with how I feel about it.

I can't explain to my mother something I can barely admit to myself.

Gently extracting my hand, I avoid her eyes and keep scrubbing. The plates in the house have never been so clean.

Meanwhile, I don't think I'll ever feel clean again.

"I'm fine, Mama."

Five

It's been days and days and days. Had to be.

I keep checking the calendar on my phone because I could *swear* it's been more like fifteen. Or perhaps even longer.

Haven't the seasons changed? Isn't there already another holiday coming up soon already?

Fine, I'm being melodramatic.

I knew that even when I made a swift exit from my mother's house after our family dinner, making up some excuse about needing to run by the grocery store before it got too late in order to escape her loving scrutiny. That moment of self-awareness didn't stop me from hightailing it home like a soap opera character in despair.

Plus, I really did need groceries today; my pantry was beyond bare. But that's not the point.

I *miss* him. I actually miss a stranger I have never met.

Now is about the time I feel like I have literally lost my mind.

I'm also pissed at the fact that J has been a master puppeteer of my emotions from the jump. Then I remember all the sweet and disgusting things he'd whispered in my ear and I miss his voice all over again.

Sherry calls while I'm shopping for fruit and lunchmeat and toilet paper, but I can't bring myself to answer. All she'll want to do is talk about Anthony and he is the absolute last person I want to hear about. I'm dealing with enough guilt and I honestly haven't thought about him since we parted ways after brunch that Sunday after church.

My cell notification dings as I'm struggling with getting my overfull paper bags through my door without spilling anything. I contort my wrist trying to fish the phone out of my purse from where it's dangling from my shoulder, losing some of my apples in the process.

Curses fill my mouth over the bruised fruit as I dump my burdens on the kitchen counter. I don't know why Sherry always feels the need to text me every time she calls and I happen to miss it –

Oh. *Oh.*

It's a text, but it isn't from Sherry. It's J.

Finally!

My heart forgets it belongs to an adult and starts racing a mile a minute, despite the message not being quite what I expect after not hearing from him at all since he left:

The Sheraton Hotel, Room 426 – J

He left the address for the hotel, and that was about it. There's something to be said for brevity and a man who can get straight to the point, but I'd be lying if I said I hadn't been expecting more after what he and I shared.

Cue the slight disappointment. He could've at least called and talked to me… but maybe he's still wrapping up loose ends from his business trip. I could see that. I just wish he –

My heart beats twice as fast when I realize I had missed the date he'd put in the text – tonight!

Holy shit! This soon? I am not ready by any stretch of the imagination, physically or mentally. The sun is already sitting low in the sky; that means I need to start getting ready right now.

I had hoped for this moment for a solid week and now that it's here, I'm freaking out.

Throwing anything perishable into my fridge with abandon and leaving everything else strewn across the counter, I dash into my bedroom and reach deep into the bowels of my closet. Way, *way* in the back hangs a dress that I have been keeping for a special occasion since I moved into this apartment several years ago. I extract it and hold it up to the light.

If I want to make a good impression – and I do – this is the dress to do it in: a long black satin dress with a cinched waist, a low neckline and a right-sided slit that reaches high heaven. Sexy without looking like a super slut. A dress that says you can have me… but you have to earn it.

Tossing the dress on the bed, I throw myself into the shower and scrub with my best-smelling vanilla body wash and a loofah like my life depends on it. I oil up when I get out while my skin is still wet to lock in the moisture. And thank *God* I had the foresight to go ahead and get my lady bits waxed earlier in the week so my lips down there are ensured to be petal soft and smooth. In the event that's even relevant, of course. The last thing I'd want to be is presumptuous, but a girl better be prepared.

I try to keep things simple and sexy in terms of makeup with a red lip, smoky eyeliner and some understated lashes, also letting my natural curls burst free from their usual honey blonde bun. I add a couple of dabs of my most expensive perfume between my upper thighs and breasts and on the backs of my knees. I smell like a snack and look like a decent catch in the tight dress and stilettos, if I do say so myself. Which is why I know I'll need my light trench coat to cover up lest I'm harassed the entire way to the hotel. Or propositioned by the pimp who trolls the train station nearest my apartment. I shudder at the thought.

After I map my destination on my phone, I waste no time hustling down to the subway. I scroll through my text messages and phone calls obsessively, trying to see if I missed anything from J.

Nothing, not since the hotel room text.

Perhaps no news is good news?

No, I'm going to stay positive this time, for my own sake. I repeat this mantra in my head as the train screeches down the track, hurtling me toward my destination – and my destiny.

The train is delayed twice, so it ends up taking over an hour to reach the street where the hotel is located. I make it topside at last, walking at a fast clip between the rows of cars parked along either side of the street, gleaming golden under the argon street lights.

Thankfully, I don't have to swing open the huge glass doors of the lobby with my shaking hands as the suited doorman does that for me. I flash a tight smile and keep it moving. If I take a minute to stop and think about what I'm doing right now, I'll head right back to the train to ride home like a coward.

After taking in the expansive lobby decked out in white marble from floor to ceiling, my heels echo the heavy thump of my heartbeat in my chest as I make my way over to the bar.

The bartender appears before me as I settle my shivering body onto a leather barstool. Dressed much like the uniformed doorman in his bowtie, vest and stiff white button-down, he gives me an appreciative glance and smiles. "Can I get you something to drink, miss?"

"Uh…" I take a peek over his shoulder at the top shelf offerings. I'm going to need something strong to steel my nerves tonight. "Let me get a shot of Hennessy, please."

After I shrug out of my coat, I suck down the whole glass of oaky liquid fire the instant it lands on the polished bar top in front of me and take a deep, deep breath. Warmth trickles down my throat and lower, settling hot and comfortable in my stomach. I lick my lips, feeling a little better already. But not too much of that, lest I be too drunk to keep my wits about me. I'll definitely need them for whatever's to come.

J gave me the room number, so I'm sure he didn't intend to meet me downstairs. I'm not ready to head up yet.

Maybe I *do* need another drink –

A tap on my shoulder nearly makes me jump out of my skin. After being so keyed up all week, I'm so startled I have to trap my squeak behind my teeth in the nick of time.

Then I turn around on my stool and about fall over in shock. And full-on, unadulterated arousal.

J stands before me, dressed simply and elegantly in belted trousers and a sweater that looks custom-fitted to his tall, leanly muscled frame. His app photos were incredible and they still do not do him justice. They'd somehow muted the sharp angles of his square jaw, the long lashes and hooded eyes the color of ancient amber.

Jesus *Christ.*

I forget how to breathe for a second.

"Figured I'd find you down here. I'd recognize that face anywhere, Gorgeous."

At the deep, velvety rumble of his voice, my panties would have spontaneously combusted – if I had bothered to wear any. Something tells me that decision was a good call as I stare up into J's warm gaze.

"J, I presume?"

I have no idea how I manage to be coy when this man's presence alone is making me so moist, my thighs are sliding against each other.

"In the flesh."

He sits down in the fortuitously empty stool to my right with an easy smile that I feel all over my body as if he's already touched me. Amazing that the effect J had on me over the phone is even more potent in person. "Can I get you another drink?"

I'm already drunk just staring at him. A slow smile pulls at my mouth, which is already watering. "No, thank you; I'm okay."

J nods, then catches the bartender's attention to order his own drink before he half-turns to look at me. As I watch him, he takes his time letting his eyes rove over my entire being before looking into my soul. "May I say: you look absolutely ethereal. Nothing short of delectable."

I suddenly feel like the finest crème brulee and bite my lip. "Thank you. You clean up well yourself."

"I'm flattered." J's drink arrives and he throws back his shot of vodka with ease. "So, how many times did you try to talk yourself out of coming here tonight?"

Giggling, I run a finger around the rim of my empty glass and avoid his eyes.

"Am I that obvious?"

"Obviously brave." He smiles again and his deep dimples flash. My insides churn with longing. "I have to admit, I was worried you wouldn't show after I'd been out of touch for a whole week." He ducks his head. "I'm sorry about that. If I had had access to my phone while I was gone, you definitely would have heard from me."

He's wonderful. *Wonderful.* Conscientious, thoughtful, kind, well-spoken, sexy as fuck – okay, I need to stop. J isn't here for a spouse audition and I'm not trying to immediately make myself a candidate for the mother of his child.

Calm down.

"Well, I'm never one to leave a gentleman hanging." I bat my lashes at him. I'm thrilled when he takes the bait and leans a little closer. God, I'm so grateful my feminine wiles have not abandoned me.

"Who says I'm a gentleman?" J's tone has settled into the same low, growly purr I remember.

Holy shit, I want to fuck him. I want to fuck him right now. It feels like someone lit a bundle of dynamite between my legs and it's burning hot, the pressure building toward the point of no return – an explosion.

My nipples tighten beneath the taut fabric of my dress. I feel my lids lower to half-mast and give him my sexiest smile.

"Who says that's what I want?"

J chuckles and I want to trace the sharp bulge of his Adam's apple with the flat of my tongue, to taste him.

"How about we move to the couch over there, where it's more comfortable?"

"Sure." He offers a hand to help me down. His skin is smooth and warm, his fingers strong as they grip mine. I can already imagine what they might feel like all over my body and my knees start to tremble as I follow him to the lobby seating area.

J smells of warm spice when he sits next to me on the comfy leather loveseat directly below one of several gigantic chandeliers that glitter over our heads. Surprisingly, we end up keeping the conversation light. I learn that he is college-educated and has been working in manufacturing logistics for the past ten years. He's never been married, has no kids, and was born to interracial English immigrants in upstate New York. That explains the slight accent that made me break out in a light sweat.

I decide to be an open book when J asks about my life and background. He perks up when I tell him about my siblings.

"I've always wanted a brother or sister," he says, looking so sad I want to reach out and wrap my arms around him. "It can be pretty lonely growing up an only child with your family's expectations for greatness heavy on your shoulders."

How eloquent was that description of a solitary childhood? I'll have to ask him if he's done any writing later.

"It has its pros and cons. More cons than pros, if I'm being honest," I say with a shake of my head, thinking of my brother's annoying antics in particular. "Either way, it would've been nice. My mother's up there in age now, so that ship has sailed."

Do I dare? I'm going to do it.

I reach out and pat the back of his hand resting on the cushion near my hip. "Sometimes you have to make your own family along the way."

His smile goes crooked and a little suggestive. "Is that what we're doing right now?"

"Maybe." I let my fingers do what they want for a change; the tips stroke back and forth over his knuckles. His little intake of breath gives me the gumption to keep going. "But I think I find you way too attractive to be family."

I blink at my own boldness. Maybe that shot of Hennessy was one shot too many.

J doesn't seem bothered by it. If anything, he subtly scoots closer. Now I can feel his heat mingling with mine, his spicy cologne layering over my own sugary sweetness and creating a scent that's ours. I can't wait to add our sweat to the mix.

He clears his throat and leans forward, moving his full, luscious lips right next to my ear. When he speaks, they graze the shell of my ear and I shiver. "You want to be my friend, then?"

I'm breathing too fast but I can't help it. I close my eyes.

"That depends. What do you do with your friends?"

I feel the tip of his nose glide over a pulse point and have to suppress a moan.

"Get beers, barbecue, go to football games."

Huffing a laugh, I shake my head but don't dare turn to look at him. The moment is already too intense. "Sounds boring," I say.

"Well, I also have 'special friends'."

I jump. Was that... a bit of tongue I felt on my neck? "A-and what exactly do you do with those kinds of friends?" I want to know. Desperately.

"Oh, those friends always come up to my room."

My breathing now consists of fast shudders in and out of my chest. I can barely see straight I'm so dazed with need. "And what do you do up there?" "Whatever we want."

Lips. Lord, that time I felt lips against my skin, soft and warm and promising. And I intend to make J keep every one of them.

His fingers on my chin gently turns my face toward his. "Do you wanna go?"

I swallow hard, my body and mind on one accord, screaming *yes, yes, yes, yes* yes —

"Lead the way," I say, voice shaking.

J is on his feet and slipping my hand into his before the words have fully left my lips.

We walk in charged silence to the bank of elevators, J still holding my hand and stroking my palm with his thumb. It's both hypnotic and erotic and I can feel myself dripping. If my dress were any shorter, he'd be able to see it, too.

We step inside. J presses the button to his floor and the doors slide closed, enclosing us in a world of our own.

He looks down at me. I stare up at him. When he steps closer, I don't step back.

"Would it be alright if I kissed you, Gorgeous?"

I wet my lips on instinct, my pulse pounding. "Only if you call me Brooklyn."

J smiles, and it's so sweet yet masculine I whimper aloud. "Okay, Brooklyn," J says, and then those pillowy lips are on mine, soft and coaxing.

Our kiss goes from tender to all-consuming immediately. We both moan as he backs me into the corner of the elevator, slowly revealing the secrets of my mouth with soft and tantalizing strokes of his tongue. His kiss has the bite of hard liquor combined with the warm flavor of cinnamon. I already can't get enough of it.

By the time the elevator stops on J's floor, I'm unable to stop myself from grinding my lower body against the rapidly growing bulge I can feel in his pants. But J is surprisingly respectful, keeping his hands planted against the wall on either side of my head the entire time. All I want is for him to shove his huge hand up my dress and feel how wet he's made me. It's driving me insane.

The doors open with a ding and J finally pulls away. I don't have to worry, though – the heat in his eyes confirms his intention as he pulls me along with him down the plush carpeted hallway. I hold on to his hand with both of mine. I need to feel him inside me so badly, I'm hardly aware of my feet and stumble more than once as J leads me to his hotel room door.

He fumbles with the key card in the lock and I giggle under my breath. Glad to know I'm not the only one shaken to the core right now.

J closes and locks the door behind us. His room is as luxurious as the rest of the hotel – all light marble and gleaming steel accents. I'm distantly aware of how beautiful everything is, but I can only see and feel J as he stalks toward me.

He looks like he could eat me up.

Something inside me responds with a trickle of fear and I'm now so horny I can barely keep myself upright. Instinctively, I back up until I hit the narrow marble counter of his kitchenette and hold on to the edge, hoping the cold stone can ground me in this reality.

J brings his face close enough for me to lick him if I wanted to.

"Brooklyn, if you want me to fuck you, you're going to have to say it."

"I do." My entire body aches and burns. *Just touch me already…*

"Say the words. I want to hear it."

"Only if you tell me your real name." I want to know so I can scream it loud enough for the entire hotel floor to hear.

"Jonathan," he says on a whisper that lands on my lips before his do.

"Jonathan, I want you to fuck me… right now…"

His kisses have become urgent, insistent. I have no problem surrendering my will to his expertise. I've never been kissed like this. It feels like an acquisition of my soul when he nibbles on my swollen bottom lip before groaning into my mouth with swipes of his tongue. I'm so slick. I can feel him hard as oak as he presses himself just below my navel.

My gaze drops to his fly. It's dim in the room, but I can see what's foretold by the size of the tent he's pitching. Jonathan licks his lips and steps back just enough to undo his belt and unzip his trousers, at last springing himself free.

And it… that thing is a rock-solid gift from the gods. It's easily the length of my arm, thick and substantial and… I want to drop to my knees and worship with my tongue and lips.

Jonathan has other plans. He grabs my shoulders and turns me to face away from him. "Put your knees on the counter – both of them."

I'm unsure for a moment because the counter seems too narrow for me to keep my balance, but Jonathan's firm hand on the small of my back keeps me steady as I crawl up there with as much grace as I can manage. Thankfully, he can't see my face as I wince at the pain of unforgiving stone on my kneecaps.

I don't think about it long. Jonathan's hands slide up the back of either thigh, spreading me wide right before his hot, wet tongue finds my dripping center. I let out a little cry. It can't be helped. The pleasure is blinding and I scramble to find something to hold on to so I can buck back against his face while that delicious tongue goes to work.

He's slurping and sucking, moaning as much as I am, diving the stiffness of his tongue deep into my quivering pussy, then returning to a soft and pliable state to work my thickened clit into submission. He glides both sets of fingers over my smooth, slick folds and I whine through the intense pleasure he's building, trying to keep the orgasm at bay that's already haunting me.

"Let me know when you want it," Jonathan whispers against the overheated skin of my ass. I should be ashamed of myself. After barely a half-hour of in-person conversation, I'm spread open on this man's countertop like a Thanksgiving turkey waiting for stuffing and I have never been so turned on in my life. I couldn't be bashful if I tried in this moment.

"Give it to me," I say, breathless as I brace myself for his invasion as best I can.

A second later I hear the distinctive sound of a condom wrapper ripping open and his throaty chuckle when he discovers the absence of my underwear. Then I feel a gentle prod and poke as his thickness teases at my gates. It already feels amazing, making my eyes roll into my head.

A deep shudder rolls through me and I realize if he keeps flicking my clit with his bulbous head like that, I'm going to come and come hard. So, I risk tumbling backward to reach behind me and grab for the whole package.

Jonathan takes the hint and shoves it home.

I yelp. I can't even help it. He's so big and it's been so long… my pussy is having a difficult time adjusting but this dick won't take no for an answer.

He stills long enough to run a soothing hand down my spine. "I'll only go when you're ready. I won't be gentle."

Well, he says he's not a gentleman, but I beg to differ. Trembling, I swallow and swallow and try to relax so the dull pain in my abdomen can subside.

"Okay," I manage to say after a moment.

Jonathan takes my green light with gusto. I hang on for dear life as his hips have suddenly transformed into pistons made of solid steel. He pounds into me, sheathing himself completely within my hot flesh with every thrust. I've never been fucked like this. It's borderline violent, especially when he steps closer and pulls my bun loose so my head tilts back onto his shoulder.

In this wild position, my back is arched as far as my spine will allow, my knees spread to my hips' capacity. I couldn't move if I tried. I'm completely at his mercy.

I've never felt so powerless during this act and I find I love every fucking second of it.

He's moving so fast. There's no sound but the staccato slap of our flesh against each other, our hot panting, and the squelching sound of my impossibly wet pussy swallowing his length to the hilt in double-time, again and again.

At this extreme angle, Jonathan hits my deepest pleasure spot like it's his mission in life, and my whimpers on each impact eventually turn to a low, continuous howl as a seething heat works its way up through my abdomen.

Deep down, I know the monster of an orgasm I'd experienced before during our phone session was a mere shadow compared to the one I know is coming for me, courtesy of Jonathan's manhood stretching me to the limit and beyond what I thought was possible for my body.

My inner muscles begin to flicker and shake around him, I'm so close.

He must feel it, because one of his hands leaves my hip to wrap around the front of my throat. But he doesn't squeeze.

"Let me know if you want me to make it hurt when you come." His breathing is heavy and labored, and the way his steady rhythm has started to go erratic lets me know he's as close to the edge as I am. "You won't regret it, I promise."

I know he speaks the truth. He says it like a man who already knows my body like the back of his hand and I'm ready to let go of everything – my need for control, my fear – all of it.

"Now," is all I say, already seizing up before he can put it into overdrive.

I think I'm ready, but I'm not. Not when Jonathan pulls my hair so hard I think it's going to rip out at the root. Not when he reaches around with his other hand while he buries himself inside me as deeply as he can and gives my throbbing clit a hard pinch between his thumb and forefinger.

The peak that hits me turns me inside out, only intensifying when Jonathan's teeth bite down at the junction of my neck and shoulder hard enough to draw blood.

I'm convulsing. When a scream finds my throat and stays there, Jonathan doesn't bother clapping a hand over my wailing mouth. There's pure electricity in my veins, shaking me from the inside out, and he's still fucking me deeply, pushing this tyrannical orgasm forward, making it go on and on and on as my walls clamp down around him and milk him for all he's worth.

Jonathan comes with a primeval roar into my neck, and I can feel him pulse hard deep inside me. It feels so good that I'm shocked to find another sneak orgasm roll in on the heels of the original and then my hips are bucking against him like a wild animal.

I can't breathe, and from the ragged sound of it, Jonathan isn't managing much better.

My *God*. I don't even know how to describe that.

As my faculties slowly return and I shift my weight, I groan at the pain in my knees. I'll have bruises for sure.

I lean forward and try to put one foot down on the floor, but Jonathan holds me in place. "Where are you going?"

Giving him an odd look over my shoulder, I hold his gaze. "Getting down…"

"What for? I'm not done with you yet."

My eyes widen as I watch him stroke himself right at my entrance. He's rock hard again and has already put on a fresh condom.

Sweeet Jesus. *The stamina.*

"That pussy is too tight and too sweet to let you off the hook so easily." "I – "

He cuts me off with a solid thrust and I'm already on the edge of coming again as we both welcome another oblivion and I chant his name like a fevered mantra.

We go at it for a solid hour after that and I can't feel my legs when we finally collapse on the floor where we previously stood, sweaty and wrecked.

My dress is bunched up beneath my titties, my limbs still sprawled where Jonathan left them: one arm thrown over my eyes, the other straight off to the side, my legs still splayed wide open.

"I didn't think a person could die from a good time, but… here we are." I laugh but it comes out more like a dry huff.

"Yeah, this is… a first for me, too."

I struggle to turn my head enough to look at Jonathan's face. His forehead is still dotted with sweat, his sweater rumpled and hanging off one shoulder from when he'd tried to whip it off and gave up halfway through the motion. He's kind of propped himself up against the wall but didn't quite make it; only his shoulder blades seem to have made it upright as he's still lying mostly flat on the floor.

"What do you mean?"

"I don't think I've ever gone four rounds on a first date."

I smile at his inability to keep his eyes open for long. Can't blame him – he put in some serious work tonight. I find myself 1000% sated for the first time in *months.*

He raises his chin. "Tell the truth – how many times did you come? I know I felt at least three."

Couldn't say why that makes me blush, but it does.

"Maybe six? The last two sort of… blended together." Into a full-body orgasm that left me speaking in tongues and made me implode. I might have blacked out for a couple of seconds, only to come back to myself to hear Jonathan's roar and feel the stiff jerks of his dick deep inside my center once again. He'd held on to my hips that last time like I was some kind of lifeline, the only thing tethering him to this plane of existence.

He hums in that way of his that I've come to associate with his being pleased with something before he slides fully onto his back.

"I think I might just stay down here for the night," he says.

There's merit to that. The feeling has started to return to my extremities, but the rest of me feels too heavy to roll over, let alone get up and drag my satiated ass home at the present moment. But I know if I lie here for too long and let my eyes close, I'm going to pass out right where I lay on this cold marble floor and it's gonna be a wrap.

It takes all my strength to push my body into an upright position.

"You could always stay, Brooklyn." A glance at the man filling the huge hotel room with his presence, even in his current disheveled condition, gives me pause. Yes, he's just blown my back out and then some, but I need the space and solitude of my own bed to process the insanity of tonight.

"Maybe next time," I say by way of diplomacy. I can imagine it is a very rare occasion indeed for a woman to turn down a man of Jonathan's caliber, but it has to be done. We still barely know each other and he could be a serial killer, after all. I obviously doubt it, but better to be safe than sorry as hell.

It takes some time, but once we can function like normal human beings again, Johnathan gallantly helps me to my feet once more. I bite my lip to hide a giddy grin when he takes it upon himself to carefully right my clothes and finger- combs my curls back into some semblance of order. Taking my hand, he walks me to the door.

He doesn't let me leave until he's cradled my face in both hands and kissed me solidly on the mouth, teasing my tongue so gently with the tip of his that my knees actually buckle. Jonathan's already holding me up with his arms tightly around me, as if he were expecting it.

He licks my lips briefly just before he pulls back, making me gasp.

"Until next time," he says with a smirk, crossing his arms as he leans in the doorway to watch me leave.

I wave and try to walk away with some measure of dignity, even though a stranger passing by would think I'm bowlegged from the way I mince toward the elevators.

Six

I wake in bed with a start the next morning, bolting upright and huffing like someone had been chasing me. An odd sense of disorientation has me looking around the space for something familiar because I'm not instantly sure where I am, but then I see things in the half-dark of early morning light seeping through the blinds – the mirrored tray of various perfume bottles on my vanity table, the flat screen TV mounted high on the wall across from the bed.

I'm home again, and the insistent ache between my legs reminds me that the wild night I'd experienced hadn't all been in my head.

Jonathan Demery. Dick god and expert conversationalist. I still can't believe he's real. I slap a hand onto my chest with a wistful sigh. He played my body like a fine instrument. I'm still vibrating.

What time is it? From the pale quality of the light beginning to fill the room, it must be close to dawn or just past it.

I want to call him. It's a desire that's borne of some seriously embarrassing thirst, but it is what it is. My whole body is throbbing. I need to hear his voice.

After that madness we created together last night, I'm going through withdrawal.

When my hand reaches for my phone on the nightstand and comes up empty, I panic. Did I leave my phone on the train? Or in his hotel room? I could have sworn I had it with me when I stumbled through the door…

I sit up and rock to my knees, fishing through the tangled sheets for my cell. Oh – there it is on the floor. I fold myself over the edge of the mattress to retrieve it with a sense of relief.

Falling back against the headboard, I find his name newly minted in my list of contacts and dial him up, even though my heart is in my throat while it rings.

He's probably asleep. This is stupid.

"Good morning, Brooklyn." Jonathan's voice isn't roughened by slumber, but I hear his sheets rustle so I know he's still in the hotel bed we never got the chance to put to the test. We'd have to remedy that soon.

Pure giddiness breaks over me like sunlight through clouds. "I think I liked it better when you called me 'Gorgeous'."

"And I think I kind of miss 'J', as a matter of fact. In this context, anyway."

"I can get behind that… *J*."

"Sounds good to me, Gorgeous."

I grin. "I didn't wake you up, did I?"

"How could I sleep at all thinking about all the many ways I fucked you last night?"

The moan is out of my mouth before I can suppress it. "I slept very little," I say, already having issues breathing normally with J in my ear once again. I have half a mind to slide my hand down lower and… the impulse winks out the moment it comes into fruition. I'm just too exhausted.

As if to prove my tired body's point, a yawn makes my jaw pop. Guess I'll have to be content just talking to J and letting his smooth tones ease my mind. I'll have to have him ease my body another time, once I get a little strength back. I swear, if I didn't have an established gym routine,

I would have passed out twenty minutes in to our first round of sex last night.

"What do you have going on today?" Steering the conversation toward less sexually charged waters would be wise for the time being.

"Mostly staying in bed. Will probably think about you."

I'm so tempted to ask just what he expected to be thinking about, but I don't go there. I just stay quiet long enough for J to ask me the same question.

"It's Sunday… I figured I'd catch up on cleaning around the house. I might run a couple of errands, too, but nothing too crazy. I can barely move." Picking at my fingernails, I yawn again. Now that the sun had risen in earnest, I can see that my bedroom is a mess of clothes thrown all over the floor and makeup smeared across the top of my dresser… I frown. I have no memory of doing all that.

That's when I notice I'm still wearing my dress from last night. I must have been more out of it than I thought.

"Sounds like busywork to me… can't it wait until tomorrow?"

It's the note of longing I hear that makes me curious. "I probably could, but why?"

"Today is the first time in a long time I have actually been able to take a break. I just want to talk to you for a while."

So sweet. I'm honestly too tired to respond the way I want to, so I say, "Alright… what did you want to talk about?"

"Last night."

Figure I might as well get comfortable; there's a lot to unpack with that. I wriggle back under the covers and wait for J to speak. I'm learning he likes picking apart complex experiences into palatable discussions, which I don't mind at all. I just wish he wanted to do so when my eyelids aren't quite so heavy.

"I didn't hurt you for real, did I?"

My heart warms at the genuine anxiousness I can hear between his words. "Not at all. I'm just a little sore, but it honestly just feels like I had a really hard workout."

"I'd say that's an understatement," J says, earning a laugh from me. He quiets and the space in conversation seems ripe for honesty. My stomach flutters with my own anxiety. "I have to say, I don't think I've ever experienced anything like that before. It was... intense."

My breath catches in my chest as I wait for J to respond. I'm going to be mortified if he diminishes my take on what we shared, if he felt like it was no big deal when I might as well have been catapulted to the moon several times over.

J finally speaks. "It was for me, too." My tense body softens once again at his admission. "Like I told you, it's never been that way the first time for me. But let me ask you something: is that the roughest sex you've ever had?"

It was, without a doubt. I'd hardly call the marks I'd left on my thighs with my own fingernails "rough". Last night his thickness turned me inside out more than once. I can already tell that I'll have bruises littering my knees and hips and thighs, and God only knew what my rearranged guts would feel like tomorrow.

I clear my throat delicately. "More or less." I'm afraid to ask about his history in that arena, but I do anyway. "I take it that it wasn't your experience?"

Unfortunately for my pride, J answers the way I suspect he will. "It was... a bit tamer than I'm used to, but I still thought it was amazing. And I mean that."

That softens the blow. A little.

Not enough to keep the embarrassment at bay, however. It drops the goofy smile I'd been wearing from my face and makes me slide myself out of bed. I put my phone on speaker. I need to do something with my hands.

"If that's your definition of tame, do I want to know what you think is kinky?" I say, scooping up clothes off the floor and sniffing to see if they were dirty before tossing the ones destined for the laundry into the basket in the corner.

J's chuckle is dark. "Think beyond whips, chains and handcuffs."

Beyond?

I can't wrap my mind around that and grab a rag to wipe my dresser and vanity mirror. And since I'm a glutton for punishment, I ask him to elaborate anyway. "What kind of, uh, *equipment* do you like to use? Other than the whips, chains and handcuffs, I mean."

"Paddles, clamps, ropes, ball gags, spreaders – "

"Okay, I get the picture." I spot some clothes hidden under the bed and get down on my hands and knees to retrieve them. The position puts my ass up in the air and makes me think about how it would feel to have J spread all my holes with some cold metal device. I'm surprised to say that my stomach does a little sick flip but I also feel a telltale trickle of wetness between my legs.

"I could teach you all about it, Gorgeous."

I want to know more, but I'm low-key terrified. I run out of stuff to clean, so I head into the kitchen. "I'm assuming you haven't had breakfast yet," I say, making a bunch of noise as I pull pots and pans from their places in the cabinet.

"Brooklyn."

Hearing my given name makes me stop. "I know you're avoiding the question."

"And just how do you know that?" I frown and slam a pan down on the stove harder than I meant to, instantly defensive.

"Calm down, tiger." J laughs and I grit my teeth. "I can tell because you're giving yourself busy work to keep from answering me."

Damn him. I blow a raspberry in frustration. Did I give him a blueprint of my heart and mind and soul every time he triggered an orgasm last night? It's unnerving for a person to understand how you tick so well when the two of us have had less than two total hours of conversation since we met.

"I'm not avoiding you." I don't like the taste of this particular lie in my mouth because I don't care for its implications. It suggests that I am more cowardly than I can admit and that I'm not as brave and daring as I'd always thought myself to be. I need to save some kind of face here. If only with the woman I have to see in the mirror every day.

"Then just stop and talk to me," J says, his voice soft and tender. "It's just a conversation. Nothing to be nervous or ashamed about. If you want me to use a speculum on you so I can lick your pussy from the inside out, all you have to do is tell me."

I gasp in shock until I hear him laughing again and realize that J is teasing me. "You bastard," I say on a loud giggle, some of the earlier tension from his proposition dissipating. Once it fades away completely in the moments that follow, I remember my courage. "If you want to show me some things, I'm open to that."

"Is that right? Oh babygirl, I can assure you that you'll be in capable hands."

I practically purr at that declaration. That's exactly what I'm hoping for. I'd be lying if I said I didn't want to know more about the BDSM world in general, and now seems as good a time as any. I don't want to lose my nerve. Besides, J and I have established a level of trust at this point despite the short length of our acquaintance. He had a lot of knowledge and sense and appeared to be the best possible person to lead me down this dark and sensual path.

"Did you want to meet up today since you don't have anything to do?"

J tsks. "So *eager*. Sure, we can do that. There's a tea house that I like a lot that's not far from me if you want to meet me there."

He's so very different from any man I have ever encountered before. Of *course* he frequents a tea house.

My phone dings when J texts me the name of his favorite tea spot and the address. Doesn't look to be far from here.

We make a plan to meet up in person again in about an hour. I speed through my hygiene and beauty routine, marveling at the fact that I'm nervous about seeing him again despite having seen him less than twelve hours ago.

I wear another dress, this one with panties to project some kind of modesty, though I'm not sure why I care to do it. Maybe I don't want to seem overly easy considering how quickly I gave it up last night. If he wants to show me these new sexual ropes, he's going to do it at my pace and on my time. My panties today would be a yellow light, but not a red one.

Thankfully, the place is less than a half-hour trek on foot from my apartment and I don't have to get on the train at all this time. I throw my trench over my maxi dress and make my way down a few blocks per his instructions.

It's a cute little Thai boba place decorated in browns and pinks, the type of restaurant a family would feel comfortable hanging out in to avoid the riffraff of NYC streets.

J is already sitting in a booth when I arrive, and the smile I get when he spots me walking through the swinging glass doors I can feel down to my toes. I'm still more than a little annoyed with him for his know-it-all attitude earlier, but his being so gorgeous does make things a bit easier.

He stands when I walk up to his table and kisses the back of my hand, the leather jacket he's wearing today cool against the skin of my forearm. Such old- school manners are such a contradiction for a man who would, by his own admission, thoroughly enjoy spewing his load on my ass cheeks while flogging me at the same time. I'm far more attracted to and intrigued by him to keep away, but rather than sit next to him I decide to slide into the booth opposite him and let my eyes drink their fill. J looks better than anything sweet posted on the menu on the wall.

He gives me a look like he's got a secret he wants to share. "Hello again, Gorgeous. You want something to eat?" He looks me up and down as if I'm the only snack on his mind.

I nibble my lip. I'm trying not to be so easily charmed but J is making it difficult, as usual.

"I'll take a matcha ice cream cone, if they have one." And I hope they do, because those things are unutterably delicious.

"Ice cream for breakfast; coming right up."

"Don't judge me," I call after him, chuckling. J makes his way to the counter to make orders for what I assume was the both of us. It feels good to be so taken care of, I have to admit. J seems to want to do it out of some natural instinct. I'm still friendly with most of my exes – they were good people, after all – but I can say none of them had ever treated me this well from the outset of those relationships, however long they lasted.

I accept my treat from J when he returns to his seat, making sure to look him in the eye with every slow, deliberate lick.

It's very satisfying watching J's pupils dilate with desire, knowing he can't do anything about it in full public view, or at least won't for my sake.

It makes me smug. I let my tasty licks take a little longer.

"So… you're willing to tell me anything I want to know, with no reservations?"

J nods, a smirk flirting with one side of his mouth. "Yes, I am. Whatever you want to know."

My tongue takes another swipe at my rapidly dwindling ice cream cone; it's easily the best I've ever had, and that's saying something. Regardless, knowing we are about to have such a taboo discussion in such an innocuous location makes me feel much bolder than I did at home.

"I want to know as much as you can tell me about your own personal exploits, but I need some kind of reference point." I purse my lips in thought.

J's eyes narrow. "I could… give you some kind of rating system. Sex acts from vanilla to extreme, if you will."

"I think that could work," I say, trying not to laugh at how absurd this is. "So what's basic 'vanilla', just so I'm clear?"

Judging by the deepening of his dimples, J seems to have the same struggle, but he plays along. "Good old-fashioned heterosexual missionary position."

"Got it." Another lick, another meeting of our eyes. "Okay. Go down the list."

J obliges me, starting off with things even I think are relatively tame: missionary as he mentioned, anal, threesomes. I keep licking my ice cream and watching him with bedroom eyes. Every so often, he sips at his boba tea.

We go on like that for a long while. My cone is halfway gone when he gets to detailing his full-on orgies with people suspended from the ceiling with nipple clamps.

I don't want to be as turned on as I am right now. It's all I can do to stop squirming, heat pooling low in my belly once more.

It's the clit clamps that make me whimper aloud. The people sitting in the booth behind us look over their shoulders in our direction with raised eyebrows.

"You haven't lived," J is saying, "until you've let someone suckle your clit while it's pinched by a clamp. You can actually *see* your pussy convulse, the orgasm is so intense."

His words make my lips part with soft breaths. I dig my fingers into my knees and wince at the slight pain, which shoots up my inner thighs and into my center. I know my panties are good and damp now.

Licking his lips, J gives me a knowing look. I take my time sucking my fingertips clean of sweetness before I meet his eyes.

"Anything I mentioned you think you might want to try?"

Right now, I just want him to fuck me seven ways from Sunday and I don't care how he does it. My heart pumps harder than ever.

"I heard quite a few things that might be right up my alley." My gaze flicks to his lips. "I can think of one thing specifically that I'd like to open my alley to."

J exhales. "Be still, my heart."

The craving is back in full effect and I am in real danger of asking J to fuck me right here on this table. "Is there somewhere you can take me?" I try not to sound desperate, but I don't think I make it.

J nods. "My place isn't far from here, and I have plenty of toys you can try out. Let's go."

Seven

J's apartment reminds me of one of those swanky day spas uptown, all glossy wood floors, cool-toned colors and leafy potted ferns in every corner.

I feel my tense shoulders relax the second he ushers me inside and invites me to sit on the couch. Despite the fact that the furniture in the living room appears to be as lean and minimalistic in style as the man himself, it's surprisingly comfortable – so much so that I don't even ask before kicking off my shoes and tucking my legs beneath me to wedge my toes between the soft cushions.

It's a wonder I'm not instantly leaking feminine juices onto my own ankles. I'm quiet about it, sure, but I'm just as turned on as I was at the tea house. Probably more so now as I watch J slink around his apartment in his elegant and purposeful way, lighting a bunch of candles one by one with a small electric torch.

In a matter of moments, a soft and smoky fragrance begins to fill the room. I find myself relaxing even further, if that were possible. I can't lie – it helps that J hasn't yet tried to make a major move. If anything, he takes his time slipping off his shoes and putting them away, closing the blinds just enough to dim the bright sunlight, setting the mood for whatever naughty thing we're about to do.

I kind of love that I have no idea what he has in mind. I'm a little afraid of it, too.

"Do I smell eucalyptus?" He doesn't look at me, now too busy hanging clean pots and pans from the steel rack suspended from the ceiling above his kitchen island, but I catch his pleased smile. Of course, I do; my eyes have been glued to him since I crossed the threshold. I couldn't look elsewhere if I tried.

"And mint," he says with a nod, finally turning that warm gaze on me once more. "I find it refreshing." His look turns dangerous. "And energizing."

I wet my lips in anticipation because I can't help it. I know for a fact he has energy in spades.

"Can I get you something to drink? Wine? Water?"

The last thing I need is to get careless and guzzle too much wine to keep my wits about me. I'll need every one of them dealing with this man. I've never met a person capable of keeping me on my toes so effortlessly.

"I'll take some water." Lord knows I'm thirsty in more ways than one right now.

He grins like he can read my thoughts all the way from the kitchen before sauntering back to the living room, closing the unnecessary distance between us at last when he sits next to me. Close enough to feel the heat from that delicious body, but not overbearing. He's left a little space between our legs. Can't say I like it, but I don't want to appear as eager as I actually feel.

I take a sip from the glass he hands me. I laugh after I swallow, having tasted freshly cut herbs on the back of my tongue. My eyes flip up to find his lips smiling at me around his own glass. "Mint?" When he nods, I laugh again. "You do tend to stay on-brand; I'll give you that."

"When something works, I tend not to change it too much."

His eyes are back to that dangerous glittering, and I know there is so much he's not saying. In the brief time we've known each other, I've come to realize that J is not a man who does things he doesn't want to do. But still… maybe I can coax out the secrets he keeps simmering just below the surface.

I can be dangerous, too.

"And how do you know when something works for you?"

J doesn't hesitate. "When I get the desired result."

"And what is it you desire?" My heart is suddenly in my throat as I stare at him, waiting for his answer.

"Right now? I just want to make you feel good."

Slowly, he reaches out a hand to me, palm up.

I stare at his offering in confusion. Um… what is he asking for here? Is this some kind of BDSM code or something? No one has explained this part of the game to me yet…

Blinking at him, I say, "I-I'm not sure what you – "

His deep chuckle interrupts me. "Your foot, Gorgeous."

Heat pools in my face and I give an embarrassed chuckle. "Oh," I say, and unfurl my body enough to stick a leg out and place my ankle in the palm of his hand.

My eyes close on their own at the feel of his warm fingers closing around my bare foot and gently squeezing. His palm is soft and smooth, too smooth for a man accustomed to hard labor. No, these hands belong to a man who rules his world with his mind.

But oh. My. God – when he starts *using* those hands, firmly rubbing his thumb up the arch of my foot and working some kind of voodoo directly into my muscle fibers, I can feel myself melting right into the buttery leather couch cushions.

I lean back with a deep sigh that sounds far too satisfied, even to myself. "What is it you said you did for a living?" I bat my lashes cartoonishly at him. "Honestly, I think you missed your calling."

He works his way through a knot near my heel I had no idea was there and a weird sort of gasping groan escapes me, so loud I slap a hand over my mouth without even thinking. *How embarrassing.*

J raises an eyebrow at me in what looks to be amusement, if the crinkles that appear at the corners of his eyes are to be believed. His hands never stop moving over my foot, from the top of my ankle to the tips of my toes. It feels like the couch has turned into a cloud beneath my body and I don't want to be anywhere other than where I am right now.

He's keeps working at my foot, quiet in his concentration. There's silence for so long I worry I'm going to drift off and start snoring, so I pry open my closed eyes to slits so I can at least watch him.

He senses my gaze and raises his head. "I take it you're enjoying this?"

I giggle. "Maybe a little bit," I say, trying to be coy even as I knew I'd be purring if I were a cat.

When J reaches for my other foot, I plop it into his open hand without hesitation.

I do groan aloud this time as he begins to work the tight muscles. God, he's so good at this…

"Hey, Gorgeous," J says, his words rolling over me like soft thunder after he's whisked me away to heaven once more, "would you be opposed to my going a little higher?"

His voice reminds me of honey and smoke. My pussy gives a little pulse in recognition and invitation.

She knows what's coming, even if my brain is currently too muddled to think straight.

Holding my breath, I give him a little nod.

J had been kneeling on the floor on the opposite end of the couch from where I've been lounging. I watch with widening eyes as he gets up and climbs onto the seat, moving my legs closer together so that they form a straight line with my feet that he positions between his knees. Crouching over me now, J begins to work his fingers into the soft tissue of my shins and calves.

It feels so good, I have to bite my lip to keep from sounding like a whore on the job. I can't stop my eyes from rolling back into my head. Jesus, who taught him how to do this? We definitely need to do this more often. I've already forgotten what stress even feels like. I can't even conceptualize it right now. All I know and can feel are this man's glorious hands moving in slow, firm circles up both my legs simultaneously. Inching closer and closer to the inevitable.

My thighs part on their own at his approach, and I'm positive my pupils are so blown with sudden desire they must look black to J from his position hovering over me, like a predator prepared to go in for the kill.

"Mm." Eyes closing briefly, he moans low in his throat after using a thumb to swipe at the hot moisture that has seeped past the containment of my panties, sucking it off like it's the sweetest thing he's ever put in his mouth.

"Would you be okay with me tasting you, Gorgeous? I don't think I can wait anymore."

Well, when he asks like that…

Who am I kidding? No part of my mind or body wants to say no to J. Not now, not ever.

With a sexy smirk, J surges slowly forward with both hands. I instinctively lift my hips so he can reach beneath me and hook the sides of my underwear with his thumbs. When he withdraws, he takes the damp satin with him – thank God I had enough sense to wear something remotely cute today – leaving me bare as the day I was born.

Just when I think he's going to toss my panties aside and get down to business, J surprises me yet again by seizing my hands with a featherlight touch. Slowly, carefully, he twists my panties into a soft rope of sorts and proceeds to bind my wrists together as I stare at him in rapturous wonder.

"Pull on that for me."

I would have done exactly as he asked even without the commanding edge that has taken up residence in his voice.

I give the makeshift handcuffs an experimental tug and find it doesn't give an inch. He's definitely done this before.

"Good." With that J rises up onto his knees and pushes my bound hands over and behind my head, coaxing my elbows into bending so he can tuck them under my neck.

He looks down at me again. "Comfortable?"

I still can't speak, my throat so tight with anticipation and need, so I just nod. Again.

J's eyes flick over me in silent study for a moment and I start to lose my nerve. He could literally rob me or rape me right now and there would be nothing I could do about it, since I just gave this man permission to tie me up with my own underwear. Maybe this is stupid…

But my doubts flee the scene when he strokes a finger across my cheekbone before letting it drift down and linger on my wet, parted lips. "Did you mean what you said about wanting to know more about the pleasurable side of pain?"

"Yeah," I manage to say, just barely, though it's more of a soft sound than a cohesive word when it leaves my throat.

J appears to understand, as his hand leaves my mouth to stroke down the side of my neck.

"If it becomes too much, just say the word 'blue'; that's your safe word. Okay?"

I can hardly hear him over the pounding of my heart, which is practically rattling my ribcage. "Okay," I say, trying really hard to remember to use actual language like a functioning adult.

He smiles by way of acknowledgement before hopping off the couch and disappearing somewhere behind me. I try to remember how to breathe for the few moments he's gone.

I feel him behind me before I see him. When I crane my neck to look up at him, I feel cool, silky fabric settle over my eyes and enclose me in darkness. "It's better this way," he says in my ear, his soft lips brushing my earlobe and making me whimper.

My sight gone for the time being, my remaining senses heighten in intensity instantly. I can picture J in my mind as I listen intently to his every movement, subtle and overt, as he moves back to his original position on the couch and settles between my bent knees.

I jump when I feel his warm breath near my center, now boiling hot and ready to blow. My back arches when he just hovers there, breathing me, not moving.

God, not being able to see him has already taken this to another level. The waiting, the not knowing what's next… it's almost too much. With some elemental instinct, I know pleasure the likes of which I have never experienced is *right there.*

My entire body is tensed and primed for it. If he so much as slides a fingertip through my slit, I'm going to come so hard I hit the roof.

I realize my currently invisible lover has other ideas when the low-cut top of my dress is pushed down past my breasts, the fabric gathering at my middle with the hem that has been rucked up beyond my upper thighs since this session began.

"Spread," he says, pressing with his hands on the insides of both knees, making me feel even more exposed as the cool air of the room settles closer to the steaming fount of my womanhood. "Wider."

Wider? I instantly regret not getting into yoga when I realize the flexibility of my hip joints is basically maxed out. J, apparently, thinks I can go a little further. Feeling him pick up my legs, I wince when he settles one over the back of the couch and the other as close to my head as it will reach. All the while, my hands are still pinned in place behind my head. I gasp when I feel J breathing near my crotch again.

For all intents and purposes, with J's elbows keeping my inner thighs solidly in place, I'm trapped.

I can't tell if I feel afraid or exhilarated. Maybe it's a lot of both?

J rips a yelp from my throat when what feels like the flat of his tongue strokes the entire length of my slit from stem to stern. *Holy fucking hell…* breathing normally is something I can no longer do. J works at my wet center, lapping and sucking, nibbling almost painfully at my rapidly swelling clit so well I swear I can feel the wetness of escaped ecstatic tears on my cheeks. The noises I'm making are unrecognizable to my own ears. I'm an animal, writhing against J's tongue in pleasure so intense it is a near pain in and of itself.

But I realize I don't yet know pain until something cold clamps around my nipples one after the other and I scream before I realize what's happening.

"You okay?" The concern tightening J's voice gives me the mental space to process and I calm myself a little. "You need to use the safe word?"

The intense, prickling pain emanating from my nipples is already beginning to refuel the wetness brewing between my legs, making me rub my thighs together in ecstasy as my desire reaches dangerous new heights. I feel like I could devour him whole. My heartbeat has turned my body into a slow, singular throb.

I want to see where this goes so badly. I have never wanted anything as much as this.

I shake my head. "I'm fine," I say, hoarse and breathless but trying desperately to let J know I'm okay with this. "Keep going. Please."

With a growl, J's hand traces a line down the center of my torso between my breasts, passing over a thin metal chain I realize connects the clamps attached to my nipples.

J does what I ask and I'm back to moaning and keening like my life depends on it, the pleasure sizzling in my bones as he works me into a frenzy.

"Don't come until I tell you to," J says, sounding breathless himself. I almost do then and there but I'm able to hold it back to extend this feeling of being suspended on the precipice of sweet oblivion.

J makes sure I don't end our fun prematurely. He pulls back and I cry out at the loss, like he'd just pulled the plug on my power source.

J chuckles. "I can feel your pussy pulsing already. Not yet, Gorgeous."

Before I can protest, his mouth latches onto one my clamped nipples to suck and tease and continue to drive me completely out of my mind. After a few minutes of that, with him moving back and forth to give both breasts equal attention, my hips are bucking beneath him of their own accord and I feel like I'm going to die if he doesn't let me come. I'm wound so tight I'm about to snap.

J can't see the desperation in my eyes, but maybe my body tells him in its own way all the waiting and pent-up tension is about to do me in. His soft lips press the softest, most lingering kiss on mine before traveling down my body, back to where they belong.

He wastes no time. He presses three fingers inside me with little resistance from my ready body, immediately pumping them in time to the rhythmic jerks of my hips. I'm right there on the edge again, practically snarling, when he hooks all three fucking fingers and works them hard against my g-spot.

The bomb inside me goes off just as J uses his free hand to pinch one of my captive nipples hard enough to turn my orgasmic howl into a desperate scream.

I scream louder with each pulse of pleasure rolling through me like a tsunami, breaking down every form of resistance in its path. J presses down on my legs to keep me from clamping them together in an effort to manage the influx of pleasure-inducing chemicals flooding my brain, my tether on reality fraying. The only parts of J that exist are those hands. He could be speaking to me right now but the rest of him is lost to the dark, glittering fog that has enveloped me as I do my best to ride out the orgasm ripping me to unrecognizable shreds.

God only knows how long it takes for me to come down, but I know I'm still tingling all over when J flips me over onto my stomach and hikes up my aching hips toward his body. His suddenly naked skin burns against my ass from behind.

The unmistakable sound of a foil wrapper ripping open reaches my ears. In the aftermath of the orgasm that nearly removed me from this earth, I feel a tiny trickle of real fear at what J has planned for me now. I honestly don't know how I'll survive it.

He again pushes my knees apart as far as they will go and enters me with a smack to one of my ass cheeks. I gasp in surprise into the bound hands pressed against my open mouth. He's as thick as I remember, hitting every spot inside me so perfectly it's all I can do to keep breathing so as not to pass out.

J's pace is fast, hard and punishing, punctuated by slaps to my backside that get harder and harder the longer he fucks me like he owns every inch of my body. Hell, at this point he does. That's why I can't bring myself to protest when his strikes get so hard they make tears spring to my eyes. I just squeeze them shut and hold on for dear life.

"Unclench that pussy, Gorgeous," he says, bending over my sweaty back to speak the tawdry words directly into my ear, licking then nipping at my neck for good measure. "Let me in deeper. I want to feel all of you around this dick."

I don't know how I manage to relax, but I know I did when I feel that part of him slip even deeper on his next thrust. J groans and I know he can tell, too.

"I want you to feel this. Let me know if it's too much."

It already is, but I still want more.

When I don't speak the safe word he gave me, J's hips go into overdrive, throwing his dick in and out of me with a power and speed I do not expect. I'm nonverbal, unable to breathe. It hurts so *good,* his pounding knocking at my cervix like a hammer, my legs trembling and hip joints burning with a stretch they can barely handle, my clamped nipples throbbing with a sharp, prickling pain as one of J's big hands firmly presses my upper body into the couch.

The pleasure is back, ratcheting higher and higher, faster this time around.

My eyes pop open. J's pace starts to falter, becoming slightly more erratic, but the force of it is still making me feel him in my stomach and chest. He's close, but not closer than I am.

This time he is merciful. "Go ahead and come for me, Gorgeous. Clench around this dick so I can fill you up."

His words start the domino effect, the gentle nudge that tilts me toward the edge, but it's the simultaneous blistering smack of my ass with the hard yank he gives the fistful of my hair he grabs that finally turns me inside out.

My lungs fill with a bellow that is never realized.

The next thing I know, I'm flat on my back and hyperventilating as I stare up at the ceiling, feeling like fireworks are going off right under my skin.

My hands are unbound and J is pressing soft kisses to the raw, reddened skin of my wrists from where he kneels on the floor beside me. I… I think I actually came so hard I blacked out for a few seconds. Maybe more than a few.

I turn my head toward him in confusion. "What happened?"

He smiles between kisses. "Something beautiful," J says with a reverence I have no idea how I earned. "You learned to let go." His eyes flip up to mine. "How do you feel? Do you have pain anywhere?"

Closing my eyes, I give my body a mental assessment, wiggling fingers and toes experimentally.

"No, actually." I feel like I *should* be in pain after the intensity of what we'd been doing, but all I feel is truly satisfied for the first time in my life. And if I'm being honest, I know it was the pain J was giving me in the midst of all that glorious pleasure that took me to my limit and beyond. I wouldn't have gotten there without it.

J's smile turns knowing just before he bends his head to press his lips to mine again, moaning softly into the kiss in a way that makes me throw my arms around his neck and my heart flutter weakly in my chest. And I actually feel safe.

J and I hook up at least every other day for weeks after that afternoon at his place. I can't get enough of him – his body, his mind, his sensual words that never fail to slide over me like silk and make me spread my legs with an ease and readiness that's shocking even to me. The mere thought of him when I'm away makes me ache something terrible. I don't even bother trying to pleasure myself when I can't see him, knowing any relief I'm able to achieve will only be hollow and frustrating. That's about the time I realize it isn't the sex I'm getting addicted to; it's J himself I'm starting to not be able to live without.

I find myself brave enough to believe he may feel the same about me, at least when we're together. Having never experienced the level of care and attentiveness from a man that he heaps on me, it's difficult to persuade my pining heart otherwise. J is patient as he draws me deeper and deeper into the world of BDSM that he knows so well. Inside of two months, my mouth has learned the smooth weight of a ball gag, my wrists and ankles have become accustomed to being bound tightly with metal and leather and nylon rope. My ass has become acutely attuned to the sharp and intensely pleasurable sting of a cane.

I've been reveling in things I never knew I could tolerate, let alone enjoy. One thing I've learned J loves to do is firmly squeeze my throat when I come whenever I'm on my back and he's on top of me so he can see my face. He was so gentle about it the first time he tried it, I was practically begging him to squeeze harder, and when he did and that orgasm thundered down on both of us at the same time, black swam around my vision and we bucked and screamed and nearly clawed each other apart when we came.

It was magnificent.

The downside to that, of course, is that the guilt I had always experienced around "normal people" seems to have increased a hundred times over. I've started to feel physically ill every time I go to my mom's for family dinner, forcing me to choke down antacids and more wine than usual for the strength to dodge all the questions my mother and siblings keep throwing my way.

Our experimentation has also forced me to change up my wardrobe, opting for longer hemlines and sleeves and higher necklines to hide the inevitable evidence our increasingly rough lovemaking leaves behind on my body. I didn't dare show up to work every day covered in bruises. Someone would call the cops on my behalf in a heartbeat.

The people closest to me suspect I'm seeing someone, but I just let them stay suspicious without confirming anything. The relationship it feels like I'm building with J has started to become precious to me, something I need to continue to function in my daily life. It's a delicious escape I don't want to go away due to being affected by people who simply wouldn't be able to understand it. So, I decide to keep it close to the chest to savor it privately. And good God, do I savor it. I can't think of anything else anymore.

Case in point, I find myself profusely apologizing when I nearly mow a little old lady down on my way to the subway, my head so far up in the clouds I didn't see her directly in my path. I help her up, dusting her off and pressing a hundred- dollar-bill into her palm when she starts to put up a fuss. She quiets quickly after that and I continue on my way.

I'm settling into an empty seat on the train when my cell goes off with the ringtone I'd assigned to J – melodically tweeting birds that remind me of how my heart sings whenever I hear his voice. My body instantly reacts. I'm wet before I even say hello.

J, having learned the language of my womanhood so well at this point, chuckles when he hears my heavy breathing on the phone.

"I need to see you today, Gorgeous," he says, in that tone that makes we want to rip my panties off and handle business myself. "I know that pussy is already good and wet for me and it's been *ages.*"

He's exaggerating, of course; it's been two days max since we've seen each other. Still, my laugh sounds desperate because to me it feels like it's been years since he's touched me.

"I can't today," I say, my eyes closing at the ache I feel all over for him. "I'm on my way to a birthday party I can't miss. But you know I would if I could."

He groans into my ear and I feel myself wind tighter. "You're killing me. I can barely walk from wanting you so badly."

"I know… I miss you, too." My eyes have already fallen to half-mast and I suddenly feel so weak, it takes real effort to force the words past my lips.

"The next time I see you, I'm going to fuck you so hard you will feel it for a month."

I whimper; it's all I can do. And it's loud enough to earn me a couple of curious looks from other folks on the train, so I close my eyes again to shut out their stares. Swallowing hard, I try not to imagine the feeling of J's sweet essence sliding down my throat and breathe deeply. I'm two seconds from coming right here on this train from his words alone.

The line beeps, snapping me out of the erotic trance that weaves around me whenever I speak to J. I blink at my screen. Apparently, I just missed a call from Tamera Collins – the birthday celebrant along with her twin brother, Timothy – and she was not happy about it, judging by the frowning emoji she just texted me.

I sigh. "I gotta call you back, J."

"Don't be gone too long, Gorgeous."

Signing off with him before I get too caught up again, I quickly dial Tam back. She rejects the call and texts me instead.

Tam: if you don't call me on video, I won't believe you're actually coming, heffa

I roll my eyes, feeling annoyance and guilt in equal measure. I'd be lying if I said I'd been as available to my friends as I could have been over the last couple of months, and clearly, they've noticed the change. Still, my strategy remains the same if they assume something negative: deny, deny, deny. Giving my hair a once-over, I call my assertive friend on video this time.

She answers immediately, perfectly arched eyebrows already raised. "I thought for sure you were gonna flake on us."

I chuckle. "No, Tam, I'm coming. See?" I hold up the phone and move it in a half circle around my head so she can see the evidence behind me. "I'm on the subway and on my way; I promise."

"Mmhm. I'll believe it when I see it. You could be going to work."

I laugh. "On a Sunday?"

Tim suddenly jumps into frame and makes a face at me, but I can tell he's trying not to laugh. "We all know you're a workaholic, Brooklyn. You ain't got to lie to kick it."

"Y'all, I'm coming!" I say, laughing in earnest now.

"Well, you better bring a good gift," Tam says, shooing her brother off screen again. "For both of us!"

Shit, now I feel guilty all over again for just grabbing a bottle of wine from my bodega and calling it good.

I get off at the next stop to find an individual gift for both of my friends. Maybe that will remind me that I'm not, in fact, a single-mindedly selfish person after all.

Eight

The party is already in full swing by the time I make it to my friends' apartment in Harlem, and stepping inside feels like walking headlong into a time warp. There's childish confetti covering every surface, lung-inflated balloons in primary colors littering the polished wood floor and bottles of every dark-colored liquor you could imagine turning the kitchen counters into a long, makeshift bar. It looks just like the apartment we all shared at one time during our years in college, where our small group met.

For all their fake-ass offense at my behavior of late, the twins descend on me with hugs like they haven't seen me in years instead of months.

"You made it!" they yell in unison, landing a heavy peck on each of my cheeks. They've turned 29 years old today, but I see they still like to move as a unit when they're drunk. And both of them are already pretty far gone this early into the evening, if you go by the glassiness of their eyes.

I hug them back before handing them each the envelopes containing the oversized birthday cards I picked up at my earlier stop. They seem satisfied with how fat each envelope is with what they assume to be cash – and they're right; you can never go wrong with that as a gift – and kiss me again before dancing off to the R&B beat playing loudly on the stereo.

As soon as they vacate, the others come up to greet me, mostly college freshman exes turned friends by the time we'd graduated – Eric and his wife, Latonya; Patrick and his best friend, Jason, both chronically single; and Nasir and his girlfriend Jessica, who is so pregnant she looks like she's about to pop any moment. The twins' older sister Cara is also in attendance. She raises a very full glass of something to me from the kitchen but doesn't come any closer. Though our families have known each other since I was in elementary school, Cara and I have always been distant. It's never been any other way, so I've always been okay with it.

"Well, hello, stranger."

I turn to see Sherry coming out of the bathroom. I don't know why I'm surprised she's here; she integrated into our friend group years and years ago. I instantly stride across the room into her embrace. I think… I think I actually missed her. What does that say about me?

When I pull back, I search her round face, hoping not to see evidence I'm on her shit list, but all my eyes gather is that she's happy to see me.

"It's good to see you," I say, and I mean it.

"Same to you, darling." She squeezes my shoulders and gives me a conspiratorial grin. "Now let's get you drunk. You're already way behind."

By the time we've devoured all the catered Jamaican food and switched from beer to double shots, I'm as drunk on the alcohol as I am the nostalgia. Our group had done its level best to stay in contact with each other over the years, but it is a rare occasion indeed when we are all together at the same time, laughing and reminiscing over the days of our misspent youth.

Over the past few hours, I let my mind hover between the present and the past, not thinking of the future at all. Reconnecting with them made me feel more like the self I used to recognize so easily in the mirror, before my wants and needs became so damn complicated. Between the booze and the good company, I felt *good.*

So good, in fact, that it took very little cajoling from my friends to get up and dance to all the music we used to get down to in the dorms back in the day, working the lacy wrap I've kept around my shoulders like the ends were wings. Even now, I'm the last woman standing since everyone else got too tired or drunk to keep up with me.

My hips don't stop moving until I look up and notice Sherry staring at me from her seat on the couch in the living room, wearing a look that reads like horror. Did I throw up on myself or something? I don't think I got *that* drunk…

I glance down and don't see any evidence, so I stumble my way to the kitchen to start helping with the cleanup since people are starting to leave for their respective homes. And to hide.

I'm drying a stack of clean plates, calling goodbyes to the last stragglers left when Sherry stalks into the kitchen. She looks ready to kill someone and I find myself backing into the corner on instinct.

"What the hell is wrong with you – "

"Have you been in touch with Brother Anthony?"

Jesus, she's like a dog with a bone.

"No, Sherry," I say, rolling my eyes as I go back to my plate. J came into my life and Anthony may as well have never existed. Where is she going with this? My shoulders tense.

"Oh? Then who the hell put those bruises around your neck, Brooklyn?"

Shit. I thought I'd put makeup on thickly enough and had kept that wrap on all night, but maybe I lost it a time or two during the evening in my tipsy state.

Gotta think fast.

"If you must know, I started taking a self-defense class. I'm not used to the moves yet and it gets a little rough in there sometimes. But I'm fine – it looks worse than it is."

I swallow thickly, trying to keep my face neutral while I'm praying my friend believes me and blames my reddened face on my drinking tonight.

Sherry's eyes bore into mine. I have always admired her intellect and I know she thinks I'm full of shit. But I see in her face that she decides to let it go, even if I don't know her reasons for doing so.

"I think you need to get a lot better at defending yourself," she says, giving me a penetrating look before she leaves the room.

My hands are shaking in the aftermath of her interrogation. I knew I didn't want people in my life to know about J to protect us, but… judging by the humiliation I feel right now, it has to be deeper than that.

In fact, I know it is.

That look on Sherry's face just before the exact moment I watched her decide not to go in on me has been burned into my mind like a brand. It's all I can see as I rock and sway in my seat along with the train on my ride home.

It was as if my friend realized I wasn't in danger. That whatever was happening to me, I was *choosing* it. And in that realization, I saw what didn't register fully until now – just a flash of it, but enough to make me feel like a dumpster had been upturned on my head.

Disgust. For half a second, Sherry had been disgusted with me. I could see it in the downturned corners of her mouth, in the wrinkle that appeared in the bridge of her nose.

And now, despite knowing how J and I feel about each other and the power I draw from the wild things he's been teaching me, I'm having a hard time not feeling the same way about myself.

A seed of shame had been planted by that look, and I can feel it growing within me at this very moment.

I don't like that it was my first instinct to lie about my bruises. I don't like that I feel this need to hide what I'm creating with J. Now I have to keep my lies consistent. What if someone else happens to see the evidence on my skin and asks about it? What if I forget what I told Sherry and it gets back to her?

I've always considered myself to be an honest person, so I'm disturbed by how effortlessly the falsehood left my mouth to be heard by someone I consider a friend. And lies tend to necessitate more lies.

Suddenly, I am standing at the top of a very slippery slope.

Is this the kind of person I'm becoming? Or is this who I've always been and just didn't know?

I groan and rub my temples. Thinking about all this is giving me a headache, although it could be all of the drinks I've indulged in tonight. I have a feeling I'll regret that decision in the morning.

My hands move down and squeeze the tight muscles on either side of my neck in a futile attempt to ease the tension there. J could do this so much better…

…And just like that, the mere thought of him flips the switch to my libido and I am pounding all over, wanting him with the fervor of a woman who hasn't had sex in decades.

Force of habit makes me pull out my phone for the first time since I made it to the party.

Seven missed calls and about twenty texts. That's… surprising, but I can't say I'm not thrilled J seems to miss me so much.

So why does my thumb hesitate over the call button?

By the time I drag my tired body through the front door of my apartment, I don't know what I feel more – shame or debilitating arousal. I toss my keys into their bowl on the console table by the door and throw my stupid wrap across the room somewhere to pick up later.

All sense of propriety has vanished and I reach a hand into my underwear to confirm my suspicions. My fingers are glossy with my own juices under the recessed lights in the hallway.

No way am I going to be able to sleep in this state. My hands are trembling. This is next level.

All business, I push every thought out of my head and march straight into my bedroom. I drop my purse on the floor next to the bed before I crawl onto the mattress and flop onto my back, ridding myself of my underwear and spreading my legs as far apart as they'll go – a lot farther these days, thanks to J.

I try to recreate my lover's special touch and sink three fingers inside my wet heat, circle my thickening clit with my thumb, roll the nipple of one breast hard between the fingers of my other hand.

I'm coming in no time, pinching my nipple harder at the apex of pleasure just the way I've learned to love, but it's not enough. The orgasm falls flat and I'm left panting and frustrated, writhing with shame on my empty bed. It's not the same without J. It just isn't.

Scrambling off the bed, I paw through the contents of my purse for my cell. J's called two more times.

I want to call him back – so badly – but I *can't*. Because what if J himself is the slippery slope? What if all this madness he's introduced me to leads me down a path with a terrible end?

Would it be better to end it now, before I get in too deep to ever get out?

Shaking my head, I ignore his texts along with the guilt that rises up in my gut like a sickening wave when I start scrolling through the list of contacts in my phone I haven't touched in months. Male contacts. The ones I keep around for a… very specific purpose.

Hell no, I shouldn't feel guilty. J and I have never declared ourselves to be monogamous. We do what we do together and that's the whole world while we're living in it. Beyond that, our lives are our own. Honestly, I should probably assume he isn't seeing just me.

I could text him right now and tell him I'm done. Then I'd be as free as I should feel to dial up my old favorite sex buddy. Instead, my insides are tied up in knots as my screen finally scrolls to a stop on his contact info.

My eyes pinch closed and I hold the phone flat against my chest so I no longer have to see the screen.

Okay, Brooklyn – get a grip.

I stare up at the ceiling and remind myself of things I know are true: that I am a grown woman, that I am beholden to no man, that I can do whatever the hell I want with whomever I want. And I am currently a woman with sexual needs so strong I can hardly see straight.

Taking a deep breath, I tap the phone number before I can talk myself out of it again. That same breath I hold captive inside my lungs, terrified he'll actually answer the phone and I'll have to see this through.

"Hello?"

Shit.

I am a grown woman. I am a grown woman. I am a grown woman.

A grown *single* woman.

"Hey." I gnaw my lip. What am I doing this for?

"It's been a long time." The smile in the man's sleepy voice is evident, but it doesn't make me weak in the knees like it used to, when we were still fooling around months and months ago.

Engaging in small talk doesn't cross my mind. Now that I have him on the phone, I need to get this over with. "I need you. Can you come over?"

A pause. "You still at the same spot?"

"Yeah."

"I'm on my way."

We hang up without either of us saying a proper goodbye, because we both know it doesn't matter.

After a few minutes of waiting on my bed, I get up and pace my bedroom because I can't keep still. Damn, I wish he had told me how long it was going to take him to get here. It's been such a long time since I reached out to him, I don't know if he lives in the same place he did the last time we hooked up. Who knows if I have time to do anything to prepare when he could already be right down the block from my apartment?

I decide to chance it and throw myself into the shower for a quick wash down. My ho dial might be a little high at the moment, but I'm not too much of a savage to be clean when he gets here.

I've just dried myself off when I hear my door buzzer. Throwing on my sexiest silk robe, I run barefoot to the door to hit the button to grant him entry. While I wait for his ascent via the elevator, I pace my tiny foyer and wrestle with the regret I know I'm going to feel by the time this night is over. But I'm too blinded by my own pounding need right now to allow thoughts of inevitable consequences to steer me from the path I'm already on.

His heavy knock on my door makes me jump. My nerves are frazzled.

Removing the security chain and unlocking the deadbolt, I open the door just enough to peek into the hallway. There Chase stands, just as tall and chocolatey as I remembered, his easy smile flashing at me in the dim light.

"What's up, Brook?"

"Hey," I say, and grab his arm to pull him inside. It had been my intention to yank him in my urgency, but he's so solid and tall it's like trying to move a boulder. He laughs lightly as he steps inside.

I push each half of his leather jacket off his shoulders and let the whole thing fall to the floor. "Damn, I haven't seen you in almost a year and that's the most you got to say?"

My response is a grunt, but even I don't know what I mean to say. I'm too busy staring at my hands as they fumble with the button of his jeans. I know the beast he's packing in there very well. That's what I need tonight.

My robe falls open to reveal much more of my damp skin than I had intended at this juncture, I'm so keyed up and borderline desperate.

"You know what I need," I say, not recognizing the peculiar hoarseness of my own voice as I shove his loosened jeans past his knees and reach deep into his boxer briefs, "and it's not a chat."

A cloud of lust passes over his face and he lowers his head in an effort to kiss me. It feels way more intimate than I want to be with him right now and I dodge it, gently redirecting his face so he buries his lips in my neck instead. If he notices, he doesn't say anything.

He picks me up with little effort and wraps my solid legs around his torso. When I realize he's heading toward the couch, a wave of actual nausea rolls over me and it takes a second for me to blink it away. No sex on the couch. It would remind me too much of J, and I'm trying not to think about him. I nudge the back of Chase's leg with my heel. "Bedroom."

He knows his way around and simply makes a right instead, shuffling us down the short hallway through the open door of my room before depositing me gently on the bed the way he always did.

His tender way with me used to make me feel so feminine and sexy. Now, though, his manner irritates me.

Before thoughts of J can resurface, I get up onto my knees and grab for Chase's substantial dick while he kicks his jeans into a corner. Before I lean in for a taste, I look up at him through my lashes. "You still working in the business?" I'd learned he was a porn performer the night he and I met at a party thrown by a friend of a friend. Ironically, I feel safer with him than a man off the street; not only was he paid for sex work professionally, he was required to be clean and free of disease at all times.

He nods, a smile flirting with his full lips. "Yeah. Just got tested two days ago. Passed with flying colors."

Good enough for me.

I don't give him a chance to sit down, let alone offer him any refreshments. Closing my eyes, I hold on to the base and slide the length of him into my mouth and down my throat with no preamble, feeling him thicken and harden against my tongue as he moans somewhere above me.

I suck him just long enough to ensure he's good and stiff before I pull away. When I do, Chase presses me onto my back before sheathing himself in a condom pulled from his jeans' pocket.

When he spreads my legs and moves to lay on top of me, it's all I can do not to roll my eyes. My sensitivity to predictability and routine must be at an all-time high these days. J has been keeping me guessing since we met. Chase has always fucked me by the book. It used to be why I considered him an old faithful – he knew how to get the job done efficiently and never needed to vary his technique too much. Now that my body has been calibrated so well by another, as Chase starts rolling his hips and pressing in and out of me, I feel… bored.

I can predict when Chase will lift one of my legs, then the other. Kiss me on my collarbone before licking each nipple and breast in turn. I know that when his pace picks up and his husky groans get louder, we won't be in missionary position for too much longer.

I'm right. He pulls out and guides me onto my side to do me sideways for a while, then flat on my stomach, then eventually onto my hands and knees so he can take me from behind.

God help me, I can't even pretend to be enjoying myself. Any whimper or moan coming from me would be a bold-faced lie. J owns them all. Chase has always been on the girthy side, so size isn't an issue; I can feel all of him on a physical level, but every other element of lovemaking is conspicuously absent.

I gasp aloud. That's it – that's what's missing. The love part of the lovemaking.

Am I really in love with J? Is that why the man who had always been able to hit all the right spots can't seem to do it for me anymore?

Chase has taken my sudden intake of breath as proof his hard fucking is getting me where I need to go and picks up his pace even further. Now I'm grunting for no other reason than he's ridding my lungs of air with every hard thrust.

Still so predictable.

But I can't be upset with him for being who he's always been to me. *I'm* the one who's changed. I'm the one who's so twisted now I can't get off at all without some form of pain being present.

I'm never going to come and be able to send him on his way at this rate. I have to do something – and quick, before my pussy is so raw from his overzealousness that I walk funny for a week without any of the benefits.

Deepening the arch in my back, I throw a glance at Chase over my shoulder with bedroom eyes. "Fuck me deeper," I say, and he obliges me.

I growl in frustration. He's bottoming out inside me and it's still not enough…

I plant my shoulders into the mattress to give myself the leverage I need to reach back and place both my hands over his. With an encouraging squeeze, I move them to my breasts and the fingers of both hands to my nipples in particular, which are not nearly as hard as they need to be.

To Chase's credit, he does pinch them, but the fact that he doesn't roll them hard between his fingers to the point that I squeal and cry out in pain makes me more frustrated than before.

J knew without my ever having to breathe a single word of what I needed. He just knew, like the cadence of his own heartbeat. He understands me on a level I'm just beginning to know myself.

I try again to get Chase to fall in line, but he does the same thing and keeps up his same old stroke, hands having returned to squeeze my hips and yank me backward onto his dick again and again. Boring, empty, basic. Devoid of everything I want.

Fuck this.

Time to try another tactic. This time, I pin him with a glare over my shoulder. "Smack my ass."

He gives me a little half-hearted pop and keeps going.

No, no, *no.*

"No, spank me – like you mean it."

Chase tries again, but it still feels more like playtime than punishment, and the latter is what I need to send me flying.

"Harder, damn it! Turn my ass red!"

He gives me a much heartier slap, closer to the sting I'm accustomed to with J, but not quite there.

"Harder!"

"Okay, stop." Chase pulls out before I can protest. I spin around on the bed to look at him.

"What's wrong?" Of course, *I* know exactly what's wrong, but I'm truly curious to know if he does.

Chase rubs at the back of his neck and looks away, more uncomfortable than I can ever remember seeing him. And that's saying something, considering what he does for a living requires no shame at all.

"I… don't remember you being into all that before."

I shrug. "Kind of a newer exploration I've been doing." Not that I owe him an explanation.

"Yeah, I'm not into all that, knocking women around and shit for fun during sex. I don't think I can give you what you want, if that's what you're into nowadays."

Part of me is relieved I no longer have to fight the inevitable anymore tonight.

I don't try to deny it; I'm too exhausted – physically and mentally. But I do feel bad that he came all the way over here and didn't get off. That's always been our arrangement, and it feels wrong to leave him hanging when he was willing to drop everything for me at a moment's notice.

"It's okay." I try to smile; sadness and regret is not sexy. I push my tits together and hold them there by way of invitation. "Don't worry about me. You can still finish, if you want."

Chase's eyes are still glassy with unspent need, so I know he's not ready to be done. Still, he's chivalrous enough to say, "Are you sure? I don't want you doing something you don't really want to. That's never been how we got down."

"I'm sure." I lick my lips in the obscene way I know he likes and he immediately rips off the condom, eyes glued to the cleavage I've created for him.

He moves a few steps closer and begins to stroke himself directly over my chest.

I bat my lashes and do my best to look fetching, bouncing and jiggling my tits, my enthusiasm waning to nothing all the while. He must have been pretty close already, because it only takes a few minutes of my ridiculous crooning for him to give a long groan and spatter my chest with his generous load.

The second the stuff cools on my skin I want to dunk myself in a tank of bleach. Not because Chase is dirty, but because it is becoming increasingly apparent that I am.

He's still trying to catch his breath when I hop off the bed and run to the bathroom. I snatch my washcloth from this morning off the rack and run the water until it warms enough to soak the towel.

I leave the water running so it can act as a barrier to the awkward silence I'd really like to avoid and call out to Chase still standing in my bedroom. "Thanks for coming over – you can let yourself out." There's no other way to say it.

Thankfully, Chase is more or less a professional in this arena, so he knows not to linger once the deed is done.

"Take it easy, Brook," he says before he leaves me alone in my apartment once again.

With that washcloth I scrub and scrub, until my chest is red and tender. I want to make sure every last trace of Chase is gone.

I don't think I'll be calling him again.

Silence in the apartment returns, and with it comes a gnawing emptiness and the shame with which I'm becoming horribly familiar.

I run another shower, ignoring the lure of J and my addiction via my cell somewhere in my bedroom. A little distance will do me some good.

Something about the sound of the water washes away my defenses, stripping away the bravado I've been using like a shield against my emotions all evening, and all I feel is a deep understanding.

Tonight has shown me how truly depraved I've become, and it looks like it's irreversible.

Nine

I'm forced to admit defeat to myself in the space of a few minutes. I don't bother with turning the shower off when I dash out of the bathroom to find my cell.

I don't bother to check for any new missed calls or texts since the last time I looked – it doesn't matter. My fingers dial J's number on their own with little interference from my brain, which is full of static and unreliable in terms of decision-making.

He picks up on the first ring. "Where have you been, Brooklyn?"

A delicious chill slithers up and down my spine at this new terse tone I've never heard him use with me before. That and the fact that he called me by my government name floods my entire body with a toxic stew of relief and dread. He really did miss me.

"I told you I went to a birthday party." My hands find the edge of my dresser as I find I have to hold myself upright on account of my suddenly weak knees.

"That was hours ago." He sounds angry and I can't manage to feel anything but delight. "How long have you been home?"

I saunter back into the bathroom, the air there now heavy and thick with steam. "Not long." The fact that I can't breathe quite right has little to do with the heaviness of atmosphere the shower has created.

"Liar," J says, and I let my robe slip from my shoulders into a soft, silken puddle at my feet.

"What do you mean?"

J's dark chuckle literally makes me take a hand and stroke it over my mound. "He couldn't fuck you right, could he, Gorgeous?"

With a whimper I can't control, I run a finger slowly up and down my slit where I stand at the mirror, now too fogged for me to see myself. That's just as well. I'm sure I look like a madwoman, with my hair wild and gooseflesh puckered all over my naked body despite the humid heat.

J is back to calling me by my designated nickname, so he must have calmed himself a little. Not that I mind him feeling a little tense, but I don't bother to lie or dodge his frank question. If he and I share nothing else, it's a naked sort of honesty that still shakes me to my core.

"No, J. He couldn't."

"And he got to come but you didn't – isn't that right?"

It feels as if my entire female reproductive system answers him with a mighty clench that is nearly painful. "No." "And you're still *so wet*, aren't you?"

God, yes. "I am." My voice is weak in response to his command over me. My legs are trembling.

"Stay where you are and text me your address. I'm coming to take care of you."

J hangs up before I can speak another word. I immediately do as he asks, my thoughts so muddled I have to rewrite my own address twice before I text it to him.

I throw myself back into the shower for no other reason than to wash the earlier events of this night down the drain. Just as with my former sex buddy's arrival, the door buzzer goes off just as I'm stepping out of the shower. When I throw on my robe again, it plasters itself to my wet body. I don't bother tying the sash. Instead, I leave it open and sprint to the front door, leaving wet footprints on the wood floor in my wake.

J is standing there when I fling the door open wide, chest heaving as if he's run the whole way up instead of taking the elevator.

He's on me before I can open my mouth, his big hand grasping my chin to hold me still so he can greet me with a ferocious kiss that speaks of the passion burning like a white flame between us. The moan I hear could have come from either of us as I stumble backward and J kicks the door closed behind him.

I'm too busy whining and trying to climb him like a tree to notice at first that there's something in his other hand, but I do when he pulls back long enough to look down into my eyes. I study his gaze and see the same need reflecting back at me, but I'm distracted when he dangles a pair of real handcuffs and some kind of metal bar in front of my face.

He doesn't give me a chance to ask any questions, despite the fact that the appearance of toys we had yet to experiment with has triggered a million different queries. J gives my breast a hard squeeze, spins me around by the waist, then gives me a light shove that has me bent over the arm of the couch in the living room.

His movements aren't measured and careful in the beginning the way I'm used to. This time, they are forceful and demanding, as if he wants to remind me and my body who they belong to.

I don't have a problem with that in the slightest.

In no time at all, my hands are cuffed painfully tight at the small of my back and my ankles are chained to a short metal bar that has my legs spread far apart. It will apparently keep me from closing them, as I often do when the intensity becomes too much.

I don't hear the telltale sound of a condom wrapper, and honestly, I'm past caring about who's monogamous between us and who's not. Every inch of me is screaming for this man and I can't concern myself with anything else.

J seats himself deep inside me with one powerful stroke that steals my breath away altogether, leaving me wheezing like I'm trying to suck in air inside of a vacuum.

With his knees bent, J hits that perfect angle to get at my swollen g-spot and I am teetering on the edge already, panting and groaning, begging him for the release I'm so desperate for.

He knows, and he doesn't tease me or make me beg. When J hears my whispered "please", he fucks me harder than ever before, smacking my backside hard enough to bruise with one hand and closing the fingers of the other around my neck.

I cough, trying not to choke when I feel something smooth and cold enter my mouth. My eyes pop open in alarm to find what looks like a small object that looks like a fat teardrop on a flared base, the beautiful color of the deep ocean.

"Get it nice and wet," J says. "For your own sake."

Obediently, I close my eyes again and lave the smoothness of the toy with my tongue, rolling it around and around in my mouth until J pulls it out again.

He runs his palm over the small of my back. "Relax."

I have no idea how he expects me to do that when it feels like his dick is taking up two thirds of my insides, but I do my best – at least until I feel J press that toy against my back door and I tense up again.

Hushing me, J strokes my back and sides before coming around the front to rub my dripping clit. I gasp at the hot contact, like metal on a live wire. All the while he presses against the plug more firmly, waiting for my involuntary muscles to soften and the fierce burning to subside. It takes a few minutes of advance and retreat, but once that thing is in all the way, J picks up the pace again.

I feel so full of fear I'll come apart at the seams.

"You come when I tell you to, Brooklyn," J says hoarsely over my whining. "Not before. Your actions have consequences."

So much for not making me beg. Another thirty seconds of this and my legs are full-on shaking and I'm barely hanging on. The impact of his hips against me simultaneously pushes the glass plug deep into my ass just for it to pop back out on his brief retreat. It's so close to double penetration I'm about to lose my mind.

"Come for me," J says, with a smack that hits the plug as well as my ass, a sharpness that makes me let out a squeak that instantly turns into a sob. I'm coming and he's coming, too, grunting hard into each surge forward past the resistance of my tightly clenching pussy. I yelp in time with the ecstasy washing over me again and again, buffeting me like waves in a storm.

J withdraws and I feel the loss like a piece of my own body has gone missing.

I don't feel bereft for long. I'm still trying to catch my breath when J's lips find mine and he helps me turn over with the most delicate touch. His breath becomes mine as he lets me hold on and use him as an anchor to the earth itself.

His kisses become urgent and insistent, his tongue coaxing mine into utter submission. "Hope you're not too tired," J says huskily in my ear. "I'm not hardly done with you yet."

My favorite refrain.

J and I tumble to and fro in my bed all night like we haven't seen each other in years. At many points, I can't tell where he starts and I end. He takes me higher each time I think it's an impossibility.

Now, I'm a reasonable enough woman to understand that there are too many feel-good chemicals flooding my body to make a definitive statement, but I think I may have really fallen in love with J a little bit while he was inside me as deeply as he could go, fucking me slowly into the sweetest oblivion I've ever known.

I'm not sure when we finally pass out in the tangled sheets. All I know is when I wake with a start, I'm sprawled on my side and look back to find J has fallen asleep with his face in the crack of my backside.

I had been sleeping so deeply, I don't realize where I am until my bleary eyes focus on my vanity mirror.

Panic sets in when I realize the sunlight slipping in through the blinds is far too strong for this time of morning… what time is it, anyway?

Squinting, I fumble around my nightstand for my phone.

I tap the screen and almost have a panic attack – it's almost *noon*! On a workday!

A string of curses leaves my mouth and I stumble from the bed to the bathroom to my closet, trying to throw an outfit together and brush my teeth at the same time. *Goddamit –*

"Where are you going?"

I'm undeterred by J's sleepy voice from my bed, beckoning me back to bliss in his arms like a mermaid singing to lost sailors of sweet death. I keep moving and yell at him around the toothbrush in my mouth. "Are you serious? I'm late for work!"

"So?"

"*So?*" That flippant remark makes me pause in the bathroom doorway with a hand on my hip, aghast. "Have I never told you how hard I worked to get this job?"

"You have." The smile stretching across J's face makes him look like a Cheshire cat. "But when was the last time you took off work? And before you say it, I mean to do something you *want* to do and not something you *have* to do."

My protest dies in my mouth and I stop brushing. He has a good point. Other than the time or two I took a couple of hours here and there to hang out with him, I haven't taken a sick day in… God, I have no idea. His eyes dance.

"Play hooky with me. Just call in sick."

My brain is already ticking through worst-case scenarios. Nothing major has been planned this week. Maybe they could miss me for a day.

Decision made, I suddenly feel lighter than I have in weeks. An entire unplanned day full of possibility stretches out before me. I feel like a kid again. Well, perhaps more like a naked woman with nothing but fun stuff to do for the next twenty-four hours.

I grab my phone and dial up my assistant. It rings and goes to her corporate voicemail, so I request to be forwarded to the front desk. When the receptionist answers, I ask her to let Nikki know I wouldn't be in the office today.

"Oh, she's out sick today… said she wasn't feeling well," the receptionist says. "She called and said she expected to be in tomorrow. The director's receptionist will also be handling your calls today."

Odd… Nikki takes off about as often as I do, which is hardly ever. I guess today is a self-care kind of day for me and my crew. Good for her.

"No problem, Willa. Thank you."

When I hang up, J is already slithering off the bed to cross the room to meet me in the doorway.

"You see?" He presses his hard, naked body flush against mine, making my eyelids flutter with lust. "The world didn't end and you are still all mine today."

"It's a miracle," I say on a giggle.

J nibbles the rounded edge of a collarbone and I shiver. "No, that would be making you come at least three more times in the shower."

J makes me *breakfast,* a sight that is by and large the sexiest thing I have ever beheld, especially when he insists on doing so naked. I make him put on my apron to protect his more important bits from kitchen hazards, and honestly, that only heightens the sensual effect.

I tend to be cold so I put on my robe, leaving it open and untied in the front for J to enjoy the view while we eat what he prepared – French toast and scrambled eggs with dill. Considering I haven't properly grocery shopped in the better part of a week, I'm amazed he manages to create something so delicious from the humble ingredients practically gathering dust in my fridge and pantry.

We eat in comfortable silence for the most part, my feet tucked warmly between J's muscled thighs.

As I inhale the French toast – so good – I have a sudden realization that I am sitting here playing house with this man and I still know very little about his life before we met.

"So, whose recipe is this? Surely someone taught you how to cook so well." I grin around my fork at J across my small table.

"I can't be a natural-born good cook?" He raises his eyebrows at me in mock offense.

Chuckling, I shake my head and finish scraping the last of the deliciousness off my plate. "Nope."

"My mother," he says after a lapse. When he doesn't elaborate, I widen my eyes to encourage him to continue, but J only winks at me and asks what I want to do the rest of the afternoon.

Interesting that he doesn't want to talk about his family, but I'm still too blissed out to press the issue. Especially when we're getting along so well. There will be plenty of time to share the parts of our pasts that made us who we are today, if we can ever stay out of bed long enough to have a substantial conversation.

"How do you feel about coming with me to a lifestyle meet tonight?"

I look up at him over the rim of my coffee. "A what?"

"A BDSM meet. Thought it might be… educational for you, just to watch."

Hm… I don't know about that. My stomach does a flip. "Watch what, exactly?"

I'm met with the infamous smirk as J helps gather our empty dishes, still naked from the back. I can't help but smile at that. "It's something you have to see for yourself," he says, heading for the kitchen sink.

Turns out I'm as good as J at avoiding questions. We spend the rest of the day lounging around in bed, watching TV between rapturous orgasms. By the time the sun is setting and we'd finished binge-watching some streaming show, J is giving me a look I don't understand.

I slide off the bed with a shrug. "What?"

"I know this TV marathon was your idea because you want to go tonight but you're afraid."

Damn him for always seeing right through me. He's right, of course. I want to go but I am terrified of the unknown. It could be some kind of dank dungeon full of overweight old men crawling around on leashes.

But isn't it better to know for sure than to wonder for the rest of my life because I was too scared for that level of truth? I level my bravest stare at J, still lounging on the bed.

"What should I wear?"

J had better be glad I kept this freakum dress way in the back of my closet, otherwise I would have had a great excuse to not go out tonight. My ass cheeks are practically hanging out of the back of my tiny black bodycon dress. I feel beyond exposed, but J assures me it's appropriate attire for the evening. He'd know best, so I roll with it.

We take a cab to Soho and arrive at a huge brownstone that takes up the better part of a city block. Even in the casual slacks and sweater J had on when he arrived at my apartment, he looks right at home among the well-heeled people milling about the palatial entryway, sipping cocktails and chatting about the weather.

I've hooked my elbow around J's arm, ears primed for talk of whips and chains, but I don't hear anything remotely salacious.

I raise an eyebrow at J. "Is this what all the fuss was about?"

"So impatient." J chuckles and starts leading me toward an expansive set of stairs at the back of the room, a row of crystal chandeliers glittering above our heads. We follow several couples and a few singles down to the bottom landing sheathed in heavy darkness, where a young woman in a red dress is passing out black masks to everyone who moves past her beyond a black velvet curtain.

J and I don our masks and the curtain parts to allow us entry.

In the center of the long, rectangular room is a stage on a raised platform. In the center of that stage is a naked woman with blonde hair that falls to the backs of her knees, standing spread eagled, chained to what looks like a gigantic metal "X". And before her is an equally naked brunette on her knees, holding some kind of device that appears to be sending an electric shock directly into the vagina of the bound woman.

Blondie is screaming her head off and I plant my feet, wondering if I should be calling the police – until I realize that every time she opens her mouth, she's screaming that she's coming.

I don't realize I've stopped dead in my tracks until J tugs on my arm with a knowing smile.

"Don't you want to see what else they have going on down here?"

Ten

Distantly, I feel a gentle tug on my arm, but I don't acknowledge it.

I can't, really. My entire being is glued to the spot. I'm not sure I've even blinked in the last sixty seconds. My eyes burn but I cannot stop staring at the erotic spectacle unfolding before me right now.

This moment has already taught me a lesson: watching a sex act live is an entirely different experience altogether from watching pornography, something with which I've had plenty of experience over the course of my life to date. Most of the men and women involved in creating a porn video are putting on a performance on some level, and one would never have an inkling of how much acting is involved unless you were in the room with them.

This? This is totally different.

J and I are standing only a few feet from the raised platform erected in the center of the room, close enough to easily smell the sweet and musky scent of both women's arousal hanging heavy in the air. The screams of ecstasy are loud enough to make my ears ring, but I can still hear the wet squishing sounds being produced by the other woman on her knees as she – oh, God – shoves her entire fisted hand in and out of the blonde's nether bits.

I'm so fiercely, intensely, and suddenly aroused, I don't recognize the familiar feeling at first because it seems so close to a pinching pain between my legs. It's only after a few moments pass of my watching the naked woman on the "X" writhe and undulate her wide hips in yet another violent public orgasm that my legs start to tremble, that fierce heat that has taken root deep inside my body slowly spreading outward until I'm covered in a light sheen of sweat. I will fuck just about anything right now, I swear to God.

I feel like an animal, my clarity of mind gradually fading as primal instinct begins to take over.

If I looked in a mirror right now, would I recognize the woman staring back?

The large male hand closing around mine feels like it comes out of nowhere and I jump, my awareness snapping back to the present like the sudden release of a taut rubber band.

I find J still standing to my left when I turn to look. He doesn't return my gaze, his honey-hued eyes staring impassively straight ahead as the blonde woman is released from her bonds by two heavily muscled men in speedos and carefully lowered to the ground… where the other woman dives face-first between her legs and eats her pussy like she was starving for it.

Guess blondie has a few orgasms left in her. I feel like I'd have passed out already after all that. I'm not experienced with all this; I know I don't have that kind of stamina.

Yet.

But I'm thinking I might want to start developing some as J's thumb begins to stroke the back of my hand. I'm so turned on that the intensity of the innocent gesture feels akin to him stroking that same digit across my bare pussy lips.

At this point, my entire body is shaking like I've been standing outside in the cold without a jacket, but all I can feel is the blistering heat coursing through my veins.

I lick my lips as I realize the scene on the platform isn't hardly over. The metal contraption has been removed and carted away somewhere, and now the blonde has arched her body into a backbend while the other woman returns to plowing into her with her fist – and now, one of the men from before has ditched the speedo in favor of a condom. He steps behind the woman on her knees and shoves his sizable dick directly inside her, with no preamble beyond a wad of saliva spat into his hand and smeared up and down the crack of her ass.

The angle at which they are rutting – as well as the way she is suddenly screaming – gives me confirmation that the orifice he's currently exploring is worlds away from her vagina.

Oh, God.

J has moved closer to my side. I know because his arm is now touching my shoulder. Knowing J as I do at this point in our relationship, I understand nothing he does is unintentional. He wants me to feel his heat, to be drawn into it like helpless prey into a spider's sticky web.

Besides that, he can probably smell how wet I am. Hell, he can probably *see* it considering how short my dress is.

If someone were to ask me afterwards, I wouldn't be able to tell them how much longer I stood there as if I had been welded to the floor, but Blonde and Company wraps things up at last. The last echoes of their mutual climaxes stop ringing through the air in the cavernous space above us and the three of them finally get up off the floor. They must have been the main attraction of the evening, because several people come to bring them silk robes and champagne flutes containing what is likely a mimosa.

Very fancy.

J squeezes my hand and recaptures my attention. If I wasn't so horny, I'd be a little offended at his knowing smirk. "What did you think of the show?"

"Surely you can tell." I roll my eyes and earn a laugh.

"Maybe… but I want to hear you say it." J gives me a gentle tug and starts to draw me away from the stage toward a long, wide hallway with carpet the exact shade of blood.

I don't answer him, too distracted by what I see. There are several plush velvet loveseats placed with their backs pushed together, forming comfy seating areas down the middle for guests to relax between sex sessions, I suppose. But it's the wall of windows on either side of the hallway that manages to drop my jaw – despite the debauchery I've already witnessed tonight.

They're viewing rooms, four on each side, each containing a couple – or many more – engaged in a variety of sex acts that certainly fit the theme for the evening. Directly in front of each window, however, is a longer couch that matches the loveseats placed down the middle of the hall like seating in a shopping mall.

It's like having unfettered access to the most intimate and private aspect of a person's life: their bedroom. And from the way the people inside are going at it all around us, they have no idea they have an audience.

Surely, they do if they're here tonight. But I have to admit the voyeuristic quality of this entire setup is getting to me in a way I've never experienced before in my life. So much blood has pooled between my thighs, my entire pussy has gone numb. All I can feel now is the steady thump of my pulse between my legs. I have no doubt I could trigger an orgasm right now if I so much as sneeze.

"Let me help you out," J says then with a chuckle and I turn to him again.

Damn, I forgot he asked me a question.

"Do you want to watch a room up close?"

Do I?

He points over my shoulder and I turn to look. In the next viewing room over, a dark-skinned woman is up on a table on her hands and knees, a ball gag in her mouth, her asshole spread wide with some kind of speculum while a man with a body fat percentage in the single digits licks her from behind.

I look at J. I can't even breathe right after seeing that. I nod, incapable of speaking actual English words at the moment. J grins and tightens his hold on me once more. "Okay, come on."

I follow him like a dutiful student, trailing a little behind as my head stays on a swivel, my brain subconsciously trying to take in everything that's going on around me.

The couch before the speculum woman's window is empty for the time being, so J and I settle in to watch the show.

Whoever runs this semi-clandestine establishment has thought of everything – there are side tables near the couches topped with sleek containers I discover are full of condoms of all sizes, baskets of artfully rolled hand towels, a selection of lubes from plain to flavored. I can also detect a hint of cinnamon in the air, like it's being pumped through the A/C system to help conceal the smells of sex. The lights in the viewing area are low and tinted red, letting the bodies writhing under the bright lights inside of each room take center stage. And there have to be some high-quality mics and speakers hidden away somewhere for it to sound like we're in the room with them.

J and I both watch while this woman allows this man to fuck her in every one of her holes while she is hogtied and helpless. I can feel myself catch fire. My body won't keep still anymore. I can't stop myself from grinding my wet pussy into the soft couch cushion beneath me, trying to get some relief from the intense pressure down there that just will. Not. Stop. Building.

The man next to me doesn't speak. All I can hear are the gasps and squeals of the woman being pleasured behind the glass.

But I definitely feel it when his pillowy lips find the column of my neck. And when one of his big hands sneaks between my legs. And especially when his two middle fingers find my hot entrance and sink deep, my soaked lips offering little by way of resistance. He keeps at it and it's not long at all until I'm gasping and holding on to my sanity for dear life.

He captures my jaw with his free hand and turns my face enough to press a kiss on my lips that could have melted my bones.

J breaks away just long enough to whisper harshly in my ear. "Keep looking, Gorgeous," he says, and I tilt my head enough to maintain my view of the sexy happenings inside the room – although I'm becoming increasingly distracted by the sexier man at my side.

I can't make myself care that anyone walking by can see us. In fact, I welcome it. The couple in the room never looks our direction, so I'm guessing the glass is actually a two-way mirror. I almost want them to see J finger fucking me to the carnal rhythm they've set.

Before my nerves and shyness can resurface, I reach over to place my hand on J's lap. He's pitched a whole tent in his relaxed slacks. With a growl, he flexes his hips to nudge his hardness into my palm.

It's me who pulls him in for a sloppy kiss this time. Our tongues do battle and I half crawl onto his lap until I'm straddling him, my wet panties pasted to my womanhood. I know the levels of pleasure he's capable of giving and I want J inside me so bad I can't see straight.

Panting, he pulls back to peer over my shoulder before fixing his intense gaze on me.

"The room over there is empty… you interested?"

I don't hesitate, knowing I'm in literal danger of losing my mind. "Fuck yes."

He helps me down and we practically run to the place he indicated, finding a hallway between the rooms that leads to a private door. It's unlocked and we step inside.

I'm not sure why I hold my breath. Maybe because of nerves or I'm afraid of coming face to face with the sex scents of strangers, but I only smell cinnamon and mint when I finally start to breathe normally.

Looking around, I see a nicely appointed bed in one corner and a metal rack full of every type of BDSM toy one could imagine – the whips and chains I had been expecting when we first arrived.

J is more intense than I've ever seen him, his eyes now nearly black with desire. He leaves me seated on the foot of the bed to wait and goes straight for that rack, quickly gathering what I've learned over our months together are his favorites. My mouth waters as I watch him return to me with a ball gag and ankle spacers. We've done this so many times, I already know to stand up and assume the position: legs straight and spread, bent over with my palms flat on the mattress.

There's no music playing in here, and I'm glad of it. The only soundtrack I need is the call and response of our heavy breathing.

He's falling on me from behind in a second flat, and I feel him plunge deep inside half a breath after that. The relief is so great, I screech at his entrance alone. Good lord, he's never been this hard before. The effort it's taking to accommodate him almost hurts and I'm in love with it.

He snarls in my ear like a rabid dog and the sixth stroke is the one that sends me flying, coming so hard I see a flash of white and my nails nearly rip the sheets on the bed to shreds. But my legs are locked into the restraints and I can't go anywhere, so J only pushes my short dress up even higher and spreads my cheeks even wider before he starts pounding my entire body into the bed with the force of his thrusts.

I've never felt it like this. He's like a wild bull on the loose. I can feel him in my chest and the force of his body bucking into mine takes my breath away, along with the subsequent secondary orgasm that turns me inside out.

My pussy is still in the middle of its rhythmic clenching when I lock eyes with a brunette sitting where I had been sitting on the viewing couch in the hallway. Despite the dim lighting out there and the black mask obscuring her face, the pure devilment in her eyes is unmistakable. Without an iota of shame, her slender legs are bent at the knee with her heels close to her hips on the couch, every intimate part of her on full display. She's touching herself as she watches us, and I can't look away as her slender hand slides up and down her lips. The knowledge that I am bearing witness to the fact that all of her dripping wetness is from watching J and I do what we always do makes me lightheaded.

"Oh, *shit!*" J changes his angle just as he lands a solid smack on my ass, and the woman outside looks dead in my eyes as I come again with a deep shudder strong enough to make my bones tremble.

When I come back to myself, still shaking with aftershocks, I find the woman gone. I can't help the twinge of disappointment I feel, knowing that I'd be lying if I said her hot stare had nothing to do with the orgasm I've just had.

There's a knock on the door, which is painted in such a way that it seems to disappear into the wall from the inside. J places a soft kiss on the small of my back before he withdraws to go answer it.

My spine stiffens as I right myself and settle onto the bed, keeping an eye on the door. J is so tall he takes up most of the doorway and I can't see who it is. I hope it's not the management here to tell us we were too loud, or something.

"She wants to know if she can join us," I hear J say, and the same woman that was outside in the hall is now in the viewing room with us.

Join us?

I'm… I don't know what to say, so I simply blink up at J. "I'm sorry, what?"

"All parties have to agree in order to accept a new partner according to the rules."

"She wants…" I trail off, trying to get my brain to work in tandem with my mouth.

"I've already told her I'm okay with it." J gives her a lecherous once-over as she walks deeper into the room.

She smiles up at him and then turns it on me. It's a pretty smile and the only feature of hers not hidden by her mask, besides her eyes.

The young woman slinks toward me like a jungle cat on the prowl, stopping just before my feet.

She doesn't speak, just reaches out for my hands, letting them hover in the air while she waits patiently for me to make a decision.

My body, thrumming with intense sexual energy, makes that decision for me. I nod and grab her hands. She squeezes them briefly and the next thing I know, she's pushing me onto my back on the bed. I've managed to flip myself over after J got up, but my ankles are still bound. I learn quickly that the space that bondage bar creates between my thighs is just enough for her head to fit.

I've done this before; in my wilder college days, I was always down for a little experimentation. But the skill with which the tongue currently working me into a frenzy is that of a woman in the game a long time. It only takes about thirty seconds and I'm on the verge of yet another orgasm.

J, however, clearly wants to draw this out. He pulls her back with an authoritative yet gentle hand, just as my hips are starting to buck.

He has us both stand up – quite a feat on my shaky legs – and brace ourselves against the wall with our hands straight up. His hands smooth over each of our ass cheeks before the thin cane I'd spied earlier in the room lands hard across both of our backsides simultaneously. We both yelp at the same time.

After a few minutes of caning, I actually can feel my juices dripping down my inner thighs.

Both of us are whimpering messes when J finally lets us go, and I practically collapse to my knees. Our mystery vixen crawls over to me and lands a soft kiss on my lips that would feel tender if her hand wasn't stroking between my legs, the same way she'd been rubbing herself when we first encountered each other.

The next thing I know, I'm caught up in a sexual whirlwind: me on top of her, the girl on top of me, the two of us devouring each other below the waist while J stands over us, stroking himself in time to our moans and sighs.

Whatever remained of the wall between myself and the realization of everything I could be as a sexual being explodes into nothingness. I lean into my darkest, basest instincts, shying away from nothing I want to do. I'm covered in her juices and she in mine. J calls us to him and we crawl over on our hands and knees to pleasure him with our mouths moving as one on either side of his dick, each of his hands fisting painfully in our hair.

When his grunts get louder and turn into heavy huffs of air, I know he's close. I let our new friend take over the stroking of his heavy staff with tongue and full lips while I tend to the bulging sac beneath.

With a moan deep in his throat, J takes a step back, one hand with a firm grip around the head. Then he barks a curse and sends his thick load streaming across both our faces, hot and sticky on my lips as it drips down from my mask.

All of us are breathing like we've been running a marathon, and it's only after I've grabbed one of the nearby towels to start cleaning up when I notice that not only do we have an audience, we'd received a standing ovation.

I'm naked as the day I was born – all three of us are by now – and I'm grinning like I've just rocked Carnegie Hall.

But I don't bask in the praise for too long. I turn back to my companions for the night. The young lady hasn't spoken since she entered the room; I only know the sound she makes when she comes. Standing up from the floor, she stretches like a satisfied cat, and I notice for the first time a tiny cat tattoo behind her right ear I can't remember seeing before. It's so familiar it makes me chuckle.

"It's funny – your tattoo looks like one my assistant Nikki has," I say, half to myself. If only Nikki could see me now.

The girl whips around. "What? What did you say?"

I frown. What's her deal? "Nothing, really. It's just your tattoo looks familiar…"

Time slows to a crawl as she pulls off the mask, revealing herself fully for the first time all evening.

The familiar face staring back at me with mouth agape looks as horrified as I suddenly feel. I might be sick to my stomach when I realize my boyfriend and I had been fucking that very same assistant half the night.

Eleven

Oh, God.
        Oh, God!
        What have I – what did we –
Jesus Christ!
Ohmygodohmygodohmygod....
"Fuck!"

Knowing I hadn't said the word out loud myself, I look up to witness Nikki shouting obscenities and pacing back and forth, seemingly trapped in time and space between myself with my back pressed against the wall as if I could disappear inside it and J sitting on the bed, looking as if he's seen a ghost.

"What the hell are you *doing* here, Brooklyn?!" Nikki comes at me then, eyes red and wild, her bottom lip trembling like she's on the verge of bursting into tears. Honestly, I am, too. But I have to keep it together here, for all our sakes.

I open my mouth to answer her but she spins away at that exact moment to snatch one of the sheets off the bed to cover the nakedness with which I am truly confused and shocked to be intimately familiar.

My assistant sat on my face multiple times. I'd felt her smooth inner muscles clench around my fingers when she came, over and over. Stomach dropping, I cover my flaming face with both hands.

Just in time, too, because Nikki is back in my face, yelling at me as if my mere presence offends her entire being. "You're not supposed to be here! You don't… you don't *do* these kinds of things, Brooklyn!"

"*Excuse me?*" The drastic shift in my assistant's tone and demeanor puts me on the defensive. "How dare you! You don't get to dictate what I do in my free time – "

"Ladies! I think we should all just… calm down."

J has his hands up as he stands, approaching the two of us like one would a pair of wild horses ready to spook and do serious damage. Which looks cartoonish considering he's still nude and masked.

Well, that's going to be much easier said than done. This is so beyond the worst-case scenario I had feared for this night, I never even considered it. Couldn't even have conceptualized it. My most private, intimate desires laid bare before a fucking coworker – a subordinate!

My body is shaking for an entirely different reason now. I just want to disappear… and why am *I* still naked? I stalk over to the bed to grab the sheet Nikki left behind and wrap it around my body again and again, until it looks like I'm wearing a toga. And I still feel just as exposed, if not more so. I sit on the side of the bed. It's better than the alternative, which is running screaming from the room.

Thanks to everything that is holy our audience had already dispersed by the time we had our… revelation. I'd never be able to show my face here again if I wanted to, whether I was masked or not.

It's only then that I notice how quiet the room has become, and when I look up from staring a hole into the floor, I notice J and Nikki are staring at each other in a way that would suggest some serious familiarity.

It makes the pit of my stomach twist into a tight, nauseating knot.

Briefly closing my eyes, I take a deep breath and release it slowly. No, I had to be overreacting to something completely innocent.

I had to be.

But… better to ask and know for sure than to stay quiet and be sorry later.

Clearing my throat, I bite my lip before I speak as both of them flick their eyes my way. "Why do I get the feeling you guys have met before?"

I sense the change in the room like someone had let in an icy breeze. Nikki instantly looks back at J, her mouth slightly ajar as if she wants to say something but can't bring herself to do it. J, on the other hand, bristles from head to toe as if I'd said something horrible about his mother instead of asking a reasonable question.

When he crosses his arms over his wide, muscular chest and that little muscle begins to flicker along his square jawline, I know he's not going to answer me.

Looks like I'll have to get a handle on this situation myself before it can spiral out of control. Nikki looks like she's on the edge.

"Nikki, listen to me – "

"No, no… this ruins everything! Everything!"

"Girl, listen!" When I shout it from the top of my lungs, Nikki stills at last and stares at me with huge brown eyes, her arms wrapped tightly around herself, trying to hold herself together.

"Listen, Nikki," I say again, trying to infuse a gentleness I don't truly feel into my voice, considering I didn't care for whatever exchange had just occurred between her and J. "You and I are both grown women. We have the right to do whatever we want in our free time, and neither of us is breaking any laws." I force a tight smile with all my might. "This only has to get weird at work if we want it to. Right?"

My fake optimism seems to give Nikki permission to relax, if only a little bit. "I… I guess you're right." She gives a nervous little laugh that sounds watery, and I realize it's likely due to the tears that had streaked down her face, leaving tracks in her makeup on her cheeks and turning her mascara into raccoon eyes.

Steeling my spine, I approach her and place my hands on each of her shoulders, trying not to take offense when she flinches mightily at my touch.

"This is what's going to happen: you're going to go home, take a shower and get a good night's sleep. Then you're going to come to work tomorrow morning with a box of those good bagels from uptown, and it's going to be business as usual. Okay?"

Nikki wants to believe me; I can see the hope that I wasn't willing to burn her career to the ground shining in her eyes plain as day. Great — now I can add tremendous guilt to the mix of horrid emotions swirling around in my gut and making me feel physically ill.

I wait for what feels like forever, holding my breath for confirmation that my assistant wasn't going to head straight to human resources on me the second she got back to the office.

Finally, she gives me a little smile. "O-okay. Thank you."

"Good." I smile back, and this time it feels genuine. Well, at least more than it did before. "Now, go home. It's going to be okay; I promise."

Nikki practically ran out of there, and honestly, I couldn't blame her. I'd want to do the same thing and probably would have if the desire to wrestle the answers I needed out of J hadn't won out.

When I turn my attention back on the man himself, I see he's back to sitting on the bed, this time staring hard at the floor with his elbows braced on his knees.

I cross my arms. "I need to know what's going on. Right now."

He sighs, long and deep.

"I'm not going to let this go, J."

"Fine. I do know her."

"I figured as much." He doesn't elaborate and I feel my blood heating. Jesus, it's like pulling teeth with him sometimes. "...Okay? *How* do you know each other?"

When I huff again in frustration, I want to reach over and slap him but I'm able to restrain myself. Barely.

"I really don't want to say."

"Well, I want you to."

"I've seen Nikki here before."

Nikki?

All at once, a hideous kind of jealousy rears up in me and I feel like spitting.

Whew, I have got to reign it in and quick.

"Well, you must know her pretty well if you call her by that nickname." I've worked with her closely for years and I just *now* started calling her that.

It's really starting to irk me that J seems to find the crown molding around the perimeter of the ceiling more interesting than the conversation I'm trying to have with him. He hasn't looked at me since before Nikki left the room.

"J, I'm not playing with you," I say through gritted teeth, getting more pissed off by the second at his sudden unwillingness to be forthcoming when I need him to be. This is a crazy ass situation and he needs to explain. Right now.

He must have heard the note of finality in my voice because his eyes finally find mine. They're brimming with tons of emotion, some of which I have no name for, but the ones I recognize are agonizingly clear: apprehension, shame and regret.

"Listen, I haven't seen her in a long time, but… she used to frequent the scene here in the city. We used to…" J pauses, clearly trying to choose his words carefully at the great risk of making me fly off the handle. "We used to play from time to time."

"I'm sorry, 'play'?"

Oh, I know what he meant. I just want to hear him say it so I don't lose anything in translation. So I know exactly how to feel.

His eyes narrow. "You know."

"Tell me anyway."

"We've been in some sessions together."

I give him a dirty look.

"*Fine.* We've fucked a few times, Brooke."

I wet my lips, nodding slowly to give myself time to process the truth. My kinky as hell boyfriend used to fuck my assistant, and not too long ago if you go by his level of discomfort in telling me.

It isn't as if I don't mean to say something – anything – to alleviate the tension gathering between us like summer storm clouds. But I stand there saying nothing for a long time, because J's handsome face tightens with worry and he reaches a hand out to me. "Look, I promise it's not – "

"Take me home," I say, not even thinking about the harshness of my words or my automatic response to step out of his reach. "I'm not in the mood anymore."

I've never not wanted him to touch me since the day we met. I'm not even sure why all of this is bothering me so much, but I'll figure it out later once I can sit with and process my feelings about everything. And everyone.

I'm too much of a coward to take my own advice and show up to work the following day like nothing happened the night before.

I have no idea if Nikki went in; I didn't even ask after her whereabouts when I called in sick because I didn't want to know.

It wouldn't be a stretch to imagine Nikki doing what I'm doing right now, stuffing my face with greasy egg rolls and kung pao chicken, all while binge- watching season after season of eager brides trying to pick the perfect wedding dress. Other than the occasional bathroom trip, I haven't gotten out of my satin shortie pajamas nor left the bed all day.

My phone is on silent where I left it, but I still catch the flash of the screen when I get yet another notification. A text or a phone call from J. I don't bother to look because I already know what it is.

He's been blowing me up all day, but I need some distance right now. It's going to take a little time for me to work some things out. After having learned that little detail, everything about my social life seems to have shifted overnight.

Even my bridal shows, which have always been a favorite, hit different. I can't muster any excitement for them, and it makes me wonder if a wedding and everything that comes with it is something I really want.

Did a long-term relationship make sense anymore? Did I still want a husband and a handful of kids – a family of my own?

I don't know, and knowing the man I'm in love with has completely shut down and iced me out emotionally has given me some major pause. Over the many times I've tried to get him to open up to me, J has always managed to wriggle very elegantly out of the confines of my questions with definitive answers that actually made sense, and I see now that shutting down is the man's normal response to adversity in a relationship. I can't pretend not to see it any longer.

Grabbing my phone, I swipe a finger to ignore all twenty-six texts and eight phone calls from J, scrolling down in my contacts until I see Nikki's name.

The mature thing to do is to call her up and ask how's she faring at work if she went, to let her know that nothing really has to change between us.

My thumb hovers over the call button for a good long while, but I can't do it.

Everything *is* different.

With a scoff of disgust at myself, I toss the phone onto the bed with enough force to make it bounce once against the mattress. I need… to just let my mind go numb for a while.

Guess it's back to the brides.

The buzzer to my front door scares me half to death, startling me out of my nap. I'm so groggy I had to have slept for several hours, all the way into night.

Didn't mean to do that, but hopefully the extra rest can help clear my muddled head.

I roll my heavy body off the bed to the sound of pounding on the door and throw on the robe hanging from the inside of my bathroom door before padding to the entrance of my apartment. Did I preorder some food for dinner and forget about it? Damn it.

A cursory glance through the peephole makes me groan. It's Sherry. *Shit.* She can see right through me and is therefore the last person on the planet I want to see right now. I bite my knuckle, hoping she can't tell I'm actually home and trying to buy time for a logical excuse in the event I need a backup plan.

"I know you're in there, Brooklyn. I come in peace, okay? I just need to talk to you."

Sherry is usually true to her word, so I know she hasn't come here to start another fight. If I can trust anyone, it's her.

With a heavy sigh, I open the door.

"Hey, Sherry."

"Hey." Her matching gold velour tracksuit looks loose and casual, but the way her smile crimps tightly at the corners and she hugs her purse to her side with her elbow makes her look anything but comfortable. If she told me she wanted to climb right out of her skin, I'd believe it.

I don't try to smile. I don't have the energy. "Come on in," I say, stepping aside.

"Thanks."

After she passes me into the foyer, I lock the door behind us.

We stand together in silence for a couple of minutes that end up feeling like hours due to the awkwardness between us, looking everywhere but at each other. I had so much I wanted to say to her after the night she came so hard for me at the twins' birthday party, but now, I don't know what to say. All the issues in my life competing for attention inside my mind have left me depleted. I just want to sleep for a year and wake up with all my problems solved.

I clear my throat after she still doesn't say anything. "Do you… want to sit down?" I gesture at the couch.

"Sure."

She settles down on one end of the couch and I curl myself into the other.

"So, what's up?" I brace myself, expecting a lecture of epic proportions from the undercurrent of resolve I heard in her voice at the door. Sherry is my dear friend and I love her to death, but I'm not in the mood to hear a single word of it.

I'm caught completely unprepared when she starts crying out of nowhere like someone had killed her dog. I'm halfway across the couch and holding her hand before my brain catches up with the action.

"Jesus, Sherry! What's wrong? What happened?"

"I'm so-sorry," she says, barely able to get the words out between hiccupping sobs. "I-I didn't want to do this. I had planned on coming over here for weeks to talk to you, but-but I didn't know how to say anything I needed or wanted to say…"

She's rambling, like she does whenever she is well and truly upset. I place both of my hands over one of hers. Sherry has been strong since the day I met her and it kills me to see her in so much pain, especially when I clearly had something to do with it.

"Don't worry about all that," I say, trying to smile. What I produce instead I'm sure looks more like a grimace as I fight against a throat trying to close up from empathetic tears of my own.

Sherry takes a deep, shuddering breath and begins to speak with a tiny voice I've never heard from her.

"First of all, I want to apologize if I have ever said or done anything to make you feel like you couldn't trust me with your feelings." Her eyes widen as if seeking my affirmation.

"Okay," I say, "but you have nothing to apologize for."

She's quiet for another minute or so, mulling over her thoughts before she speaks again.

"That may be, but I know you are in some kind of relationship where your, uh, partner is getting physical with you – and don't try to deny it; I've seen the evidence. I… it just hurts me that at some point I made you feel like you couldn't trust me."

What the hell is she talking about? Abuse?

Realization dawns and I feel a little sick to my stomach. With everything going on, I'd forgotten.

She's talking about the bruises she saw at the party.

"Sherry, it's not – "

"I know you're going to say it's nothing, that it's not a big deal, but if someone is hurting you, I *will* call the police on his ass, understand?"

Oh, Sherry. I love her so. She's so far off, it would almost be funny if she wasn't clearly so upset. I reach out my arms and hug her tightly, letting out a silent sigh of release when she returns my pressure.

"Listen," I say as I pull back, "I promise you I'm okay and it is not at all what you think."

Her brown eyes still glisten, but at least she's stopped crying. Sherry squares her shoulders like she's preparing to receive marching orders. "I promise I'll listen if you want to tell me. No judgment."

Man, am I glad to hear that.

And just like that, I recognize the moment I hadn't realized I had been waiting for since before I met J: I could unburden myself completely if I was brave enough.

So, I decide that I am. I tell her about everything, from fantasizing at church, to the BDSM app, to the ins and out of my relationship with J. I don't mention the great mishap with Nikki in order to protect her privacy, but I give the info to my friend as raw as she can stand it.

To her credit, Sherry only gasps twice. I did more than that at the BDSM group the night before.

"Well," she says when I finish, looking dazed. "I hadn't expected you to say any of that."

"I know. That's why I was so scared to tell you. I knew what you would think of me after that." I can't help but hang my head. This is likely the last conversation we'll have as friends. Our lifestyles are just incompatible.

"What I would think? You mean that you are a complex person with complex desires and that you're still my friend?"

Tears spring to my eyes before I can hold them back. "Really?"

"Really." She smiles and it's as bright as it's ever been. "Your life is your life, Brooklyn. I just wanted to know you're happy *and* safe."

I'm crying for real now, tears falling like I've sprung a leak.

Even with everything I'm going through and everything I've learned that I am, I still have a friend.

Twelve

When I wake up the next morning, I feel like a new human being altogether.

Sherry stayed over for hours and we talked and talked; once I started and saw how understanding she could be, I couldn't stop. She only went home a couple of hours ago and I am dog tired, but happier than I've felt in longer than I could even remember. It felt like a gigantic boulder disappeared from my chest while I was sleeping and now I could breathe again.

The only thing that could make me feel even better is to talk through my issues with J. There's nothing I want more.

He picks up on the second ring instead of the first like normal. I feel a way about that, but I don't make a fuss. If I was in my feelings the other night, he had a right to still be in his.

After my lengthy conversation with Sherry, I feel too empowered to mince words. "I think we should talk about the other night."

That sigh again. I'm starting to find that I'm getting tired of hearing it. "I know. You sure you want to do this now, before you have to go to work and will probably see her?"

I must have pushed Nikki so far from my mind after our semi-traumatic shared experience, I literally forgot that the likelihood of my running into her this morning was exponentially high.

My stomach twists painfully. "Shit. I forgot about that."

"Listen," J says, the clear reluctance in his words making me clench my teeth. "I'm sorry I wasn't very open about my dealings with her. It's just… my situation with her got very awkward well before you and I ever met, and I didn't want you drawn into the type of drama she tends to be part of."

I frown at the phone. "What kind of drama are you talking about?"

"The kind that could make your work environment very uncomfortable, but that's why I didn't want to poison the well if you've never had that kind of experience with her."

Now, I'm just intrigued. What in the world had happened between those two that had clearly put such a bad taste in J's mouth when it came to Nikki?

Fortunately for him, I didn't have time to ask about details. I had to get ready for work and haul ass to the subway at this point in the morning to make it on time.

"Well, since you've apparently dealt with her on a more personal level than I have, how do you suggest I deal with her moving forward?"

J gives a thought pause. "Like you told her, you're both adults who have the right to do whatever they want with whomever they want. You don't have to talk about it. Just own it. You don't have anything to be ashamed of."

I smile despite the fact that J can't see it, but I hope he can at least hear it in my voice. "I appreciate that, J."

At least four separate times on the ride to work I seriously considered getting off on a random stop and wandering my way back to my apartment, but the adult in me wins out and I drag myself into my office building on lead feet.

Nikki is nowhere around when I slink down the long hallway to my office, and the lack of notes on my desk indicates she hasn't broached my door.

You know what? Better to nip this weirdness in the bud right now. I'm going to go find *her.*

I suspect she's hiding since it takes a real effort to track her down, having searched the women's restroom, the breakroom, and the smaller breakout room offices. I have her cornered when I head down the back stairs to the former smoke break area and find her standing at the bottom of the stairwell, fiddling with her cell phone.

She looks up at me like I am death incarnate coming to snatch her soul away. I don't think I've ever inspired that level of fear in anyone before, but I can't say I like it.

Her eyes go round as saucers. "You're coming to fire me, aren't you?"

"What? Why in the world would I fire you?" Even I have to admit my heels click ominously against the chipped, dirty tile.

Her face screws up as if the answer would have been obviously to a two- year-old. "Because of – "

"Nikki, your career is not in jeopardy, no matter what you might think. I'd know. Even if I felt like opening up the company to a wrongful termination suit, you haven't done anything wrong. "

I have to admit, it's beyond satisfying watching the worry drain away from her face. Her eyes close and it looks like she's trying to fight back tears.

"God… I've been so worried about that. I'm so sorry about the other night, Brooklyn. You have no idea."

I chuckle darkly at that. "I think I might." I brace my shoulder on the wall a few feet away from her and she smiles. "Listen, we're both professionals who take our jobs seriously and do them well. Our work and personal lives are still separate, even if they unintentionally mingled briefly. There's no reason why we can't *stay* professional."

Nikki's bright smile lights up the gloomy hallway. "You're right. Thank you, Brooklyn. I won't forget it."

"Of course."

As she heads back up the stairs before I do, I can't help but ask the question that has been burning in my mind since that night, one J still hasn't answered to my satisfaction. "Oh, Nikki…"

She looks down at me over her shoulder. "Yes, boss?"

I falter for a second, not wanting to freak her out, but my morbid curiosity takes over. "Um… how exactly did you meet J?"

The relative darkness in the stairwell still can't hide the blush that stains Nikki's cheeks. "We moved in the same circles in… in that world. We would partner a lot."

"Oh," I say, my own smile dimming, "okay."

I stay down there for a few minutes after she's gone, gnawing on the knowledge that I'm not experiencing the same feeling I had when J gave me his own vague version of the nature of their former relationship. Neither one of them was telling me everything.

Still, I don't broach the issue again with J when he calls me around lunchtime to invite me over to his place for dinner. Apparently, he wants to cook for me, a real first. I suppose that's his way of making a nice gesture when he knows he messed up. So, I let him make it up to me, even though he doesn't admit that's what he's doing. Doesn't mean I can't enjoy it.

Of course, J has exquisite taste in wine and food. The filet mignon he grills for us is cooked to medium rare perfection, as are the garlic mashed potatoes and asparagus, and the Chablis dances across my palate.

Still, I notice he's not as free-flowing with conversation as he normally is, so I take it upon myself to prod him along.

"So, you've never told me who taught you to cook so well." I grin at him over my wineglass.

His own smile doesn't quite meet his eyes and makes mine wither on the vine. "My mother…remember? She was an excellent cook."

He keeps chewing and doesn't elaborate. I roll my wrist to encourage him to continue, but he just reaches for the wine with that trademark smirk and tops me off.

A couple of months ago, I might have found his closed demeanor a refreshing challenge in getting him to open up to me, to maybe even clear the way to falling in love. Now? I'm just irritated.

Reason being is that I've come to know this is a pattern of behavior for J. In my mind, we've crossed so many physical and emotional chasms together, I feel closer to him than to anyone else in my life, perhaps ever. But if I'm telling myself the God's honest truth, I know as much about J as I did when we met months ago, while I have been laid bare before him in every possible way.

He's asked me to trust him, and I did – intrinsically. But he still couldn't place the same faith in me, even now?

J has withdrawn in a major emotional way, but nothing has changed if you let him tell it. I know it has, but I can't understand why.

I let him take the lead in the conversation, steering it to the much safer waters of news and current events, and I start to tune out.

What if this is all there is? What if this is all J will ever be capable of, borderline meaningless chit chat on everything except sex? How will I feel if this is confirmation that kinky sex is our only real connection? Could I really be nourished by a relationship like that?

"You never did tell me what you thought of the BDSM party night," J says then, proving the point I'd just made in my mind.

It was… earth-shattering. Transformative. But I say, "I liked it a lot. Up until, you know, the very end." It still makes me blush to know I've had my assistant's pussy in my face, a woman I've learned is sweet in more ways than one.

J chuckles. "Understandable. What did she say when you talked to her?"

I quickly relay the tale of our clandestine meetup in the forgotten service hallway and he nods with apparent satisfaction of its resolution. "I'm glad you got in front of it," he says.

"Me, too."

He peers at me for a second as he pushes his now-empty plate toward the center of the table.

"Do you think you'd want to go back?"

"To a 'party'?"

Why is he suddenly smiling so hard?

I opt for the truth. "I definitely would. To the next one on the calendar, even."

"Good." J's broad shoulders relax further, presumably due to the fact that our conversation is no longer in personal territory. Sex and depravity are clearly his comfort zone. "Lucky for you, there's another one on schedule for tonight."

With my consent in the bag, J fancies himself my personal tour guide to the world of underground BDSM events, taking me with him to as many as he can fit into his busy work schedule and mine. I make every effort to try one or two new things every time I go – hot wax on intimate areas, bigger and bigger insertions into more of my body's openings, even a time or two strapped to the "X".

Every time, I push myself further and harder with J's constant encouragement. Each time I reach sexual heights the likes of which I never knew existed.

After my deep conversation with Sherry and the lifting of that heavy burden of guilt and shame at my unusual lifestyle, I feel freer to indulge my every whim and desire than I ever did before. I'm a little more transformed after each visit. I find myself standing a little taller, being a little more assertive on the street. I have no idea who the person is that I'm becoming, but I welcome all of her edginess and sass and outright boldness.

I think I might like this new version of myself that's beginning to emerge.

I was becoming fearless.

I'm certain that's true after a couple of months, when I have over twenty events under my belt thanks to J's assistance and guidance. By this point, there have been so many moments in which my man was so tender and gentle with me, I knew there had to be some real emotional affection there; no one was such an excellent actor at all times.

Despite my general irritation with J's difficulties with emotionality, he's spent so much time with me at my most vulnerable and vocalized how beautiful he found it that I knew beyond all doubt that I was falling in love with him in a real way. Flaws and all.

And I plan to tell him so to his face so there would be no doubt of how I feel about him.

It's my turn to prepare dinner this week anyway, so it's no difficult feat to get him to my house. I wine and dine him just as he's done for me so many times since we met, then once he's good and relaxed, I hit him with the question I know will clear a path for my confession.

I keep it playful and light, not even looking at him when I say it. "So... how did you know you were in love in the past?"

Regret blooms in my chest instantly when I see the look on his face, like he'd been suddenly stripped naked in public and has nowhere to hide.

"Why the fuck would you ask me that?" J's voice is low and dangerous in a way that's nearly scary.

My jaw drops and I shrink away from him, shocked to my core. He's never spoken to me that way. Not once.

"I-I'm sorry – it was just a question – "

"Jesus..." J stands with a movement so sudden it knocks over his chair and he stalks away from the table into the kitchen.

"Hey! What is your problem?" Have discussions of love always been this triggering for him and I missed it? He looks to be in clear distress of some kind as he runs water over his hands before clawing them through his hair before bracing himself on the sink.

That is not at all the reaction I expected, and now I'm glad I didn't say my piece. "J – "

"I don't want to talk about that right now, alright?" He looks over his shoulder at me, and I soften a bit when I see real sadness in his eyes. "I'm sorry. I didn't mean to react like that, but – I'm sorry. Okay?"

"Fine," I say with a shrug, standing myself to clear our plates from the table.

I don't bring it up again.

The Brooklyn at the beginning of the year would have sulked for months at J's reaction to the love question. The Brooklyn of now has learned to roll with the romantic punches because she has better things to do.

If I thought J was pretending not to be pulling away from the relationship, I confirmed as much when the frequency of our joint BDSM club visits were cut by half almost overnight. Suddenly, J had so much work to do. Now, he's frequently out of town on business or stuck at his office with a difficult client.

That never used to stop his fun before, but I don't say anything about it beyond wishing him well and making plans for the next meetup.

At first, I stayed home when J wouldn't make time to go with me, but I figured out pretty quick how to navigate things in that world all on my own. I was shaking from head to toe the first time I dared to do it, but everyone was so accommodating and lusty for me, I felt like a fucking goddess by the time I dragged myself home. I kept seeing those same people each time I went back without J and found I was actually making friends. I exchanged numbers with a handful of them, and the next thing I knew, I had buddies of both sexes willing to hold my hand while someone else used the mechanical thrusting machine on my asshole.

It was wild and decadent. I loved every second of it, and shock of all shocks? I found I didn't think about J as much when he wasn't around.

When that timeframe begins to get longer and longer, I compensate by going to the club more and more often alone. I call Sherry and tell her about all my sordid adventures and she eats it all up. The atmosphere at work gets more relaxed between myself and Nikki; though we still avoid each other at BDSM events, we still felt comfortable enough to mention surface-level experiences to each other in passing.

I wake up one morning and realize it's not J I'm dreaming of anymore when I'm home alone in my bed. It's the energy in the club, the high than can only come from multiple strangers-turned-lovers reaching the height of ecstasy and pain simultaneously, together. I can't get enough of it. It feeds my soul in a way I never could have anticipated when I go alone.

Which is why I've taken to turning my cell off altogether once the real festivities start so my night can be free from distractions, a big departure from the way I held on to it like a lifeline when I first began this journey.

I'm wearing latex tonight in the form of a cherry red corset and skirt that barely covers my ass. I don't feel the barest hint of embarrassment about my outfits anymore, either.

My phone rings just as I pull it out of my purse to turn it off and complete my ritual for the night, and I can't lie, my heart literally skips a beat.

It's J.

By now it's been, what, three weeks since I've heard from him at all? According to our last conversation, he was going on some kind of retreat with his business partners in some remote area of the world where he would be unreachable, but I don't put much stock in that excuse. After all, that's what it is – a reason to avoid intimacy. He collects them like seashells and I'm tired of it.

I don't know why I answer, but I do.

"Hello?"

"Hey, Gorgeous."

I'd be lying outright if I said that deep voice and that nickname still doesn't make my toes curl.

"Hi, J. Can I call you back? I'm in the middle of something."

"I know. I'm here, too."

What?

My head is instantly turning, searching for him.

"I'm at the bar. I just need to talk to you for a minute. Please?"

How can a woman possible say no to that?

A minute later, I find him exactly where he said he'd be, looking impossibly delicious in a black blazer and maroon pants.

He's saved me a seat, so I sit down delicately to mind my outfit. "Didn't expect to see you here."

J stares like he's never seen me before. "God, you... you look incredible."

I order myself not to blush. "Thank you. You said you wanted to talk?"

"Oh... yeah, I did." He glances away as if uncomfortable and I half expect him to bolt for the door from the expression on his face. "I've never been in love before."

I stare. "Okay…"

"That's the answer to the question you asked me when I was at your house. And no, I haven't."

So, love is a foreign emotion to him entirely? That's a lot to unpack and I certainly don't have time to do it right now.

"Thank you for telling me."

"I did because I want you to know the feelings that I've been having for you I have been struggling with because I have never felt them for another woman in my life. It scared me to death. I've never felt like I've needed someone in a real way before and… and I handled it badly. I'm sorry about that."

My chest warms when he takes my gloved hand and gently presses his lips to my knuckles. I swallow hard, then smile. "I forgive you."

"Good. And I also want you to know that I want to try for something real – something lasting – with you."

My arched eyebrows nearly hit my hairline. Is this a *proposal?*

I don't have time to pick it apart to determine what *kind* of proposal it is. Just then, the small group of people I've befriended over the last few weeks walks up to us, greeting J briefly before they all turn to me.

"Brooklyn! You look fabulous. Are you ready to go downstairs? It's double monster dildo night for the ladies!"

I look from the smiling group I've made for myself and back at J, looking a little forlorn as he waits.

I'd be lying if I said J doesn't have a piece of my heart – he absolutely does. I can see us exploring something real, as he said, and potentially enjoying every aspect that kind of life has to offer.

On the other hand, I feel more myself indulging in the activities in this establishment on my own than I ever have in my life, and that might be worth exploring, too.

I nibble my lip, my chest aching as I look back and forth from my people to my man.

Why does this feel like a decision I can't come back from?

ABOUT THE AUTHOR

Brooke Dean is a mother, storyteller, content creator, producer, editorial operations manager - and now author - with over 20 years of television and digital media experience having worked at MSNBC, A+E Television Networks and Audible, Inc. A native Philadelphian now a New York City transplant, Brooke currently resides in Queens with her son Jaxon, who is also the author of the children's book series *The Whisker Gang*.

www.brookeddean.com

IG @brookedeanauthor